COMMON OR GARDEN VARIETY HEROES

Also by Alexandria Blaelock

FICTION
That Love Nonsense

MS BLAELOCK'S BOOKS
Stress Free Dinner Parties
Signature Wardrobe Planning
Holistic Personal Finance
Minimally Viable Housekeeping

SHORT STORY COLLECTIONS
The Haunting of Hayward Hall

SHORT STORIES
Alma's Grace
Balancing the Book
Bygone Boyfriend
Carmelita Basingstoke
Fate in Your Hands
Kiss of Death
Lady of the Looking Glass
Life in the Security Directorate
Long Weekend in the Snow
Love in the Security Directorate
Morning Star, Evening Star, Superstar
Needy Bitch
Payton's Run
Phoenix Child
Secret Singer
Shining Star
Ship in a Bottle
Simone Says Hands in the Air
The Day the Schedule Broke
The Guardian's Vigil

COMMON OR GARDEN VARIETY HEROES

ALEXANDRIA BLAELOCK

Bluemere Books
MELBOURNE, AUSTRALIA

Ordering Information:
Discounts are available on quantity purchases. For details, contact orders@bluemerebooks.com.

Common or Garden Variety Heroes/Alexandria Blaelock
hardback ISBN: 978-1-925749-67-0
paperback ISBN: 978-1-925749-68-7
digital ISBN: 978-1-925749-69-4

Book Layout © BookDesignTemplates.com

Contents

INTRODUCTION

About one hundred years ago, I went on strike. At that time, my employer was proposing to abandon annual inflation-based pay rises and introduce productivity-based pay rises instead.

Theoretically, they're the kind where you get a small percentage of the profits the business made that year.

I can't honestly say that I thought much further than taking a day off work and doing something fun, though the memory of what I did has receded even further than the memory of taking the day off.

But I can still remember the essence of what my friend Linda said at the time, and it's stuck with me ever since.

It was something along the lines of the people who came into work and did their work, day in and day out were the real heroes.

The thankless ones who never heard anyone say "good job," or "thanks."

They were the ones who deserved the payrises, not the executives who'd be the ones actually taking them under the new system.

She was right.

My employers got their way, and when the time came for the annual pay rise, I didn't get one.

Because my job was basically to do what I was told.

My job just didn't have the scope to do anything that might lead to a pay rise.

And it wasn't just me, employers everywhere were moving towards productivity pay rises.

Eventually I left that place, got an education, and more in the way of bargaining power.

But I never forgot what Linda said.

We've just come through the kind of year that academics are going to be talking about for decades. And we're heading into another one.

And Linda is still right.

All those people working in supermarkets, and petrol stations.

All the people delivering take-out dinners and boxes of vegetables.

All those people mopping the floors in hospitals and aged care facilities.

They're the real heroes, and they're still the worst paid.

So for this collection of five short stories, I've tried to imagine ordinary people, thrust into extraordinary circumstances.

And because every universe needs someone to clean up after the superheroes have done their work and moved onto the the pub to celebrate, I've included science fiction, fantasy, mystery and romance.

Starting with Gemma Jones, in remission, forced to take her leave entitlements.

Vee, who just wants a quiet life on Mephisto station, but is drafted into the Jade Dragon Justiciary.

Rosa Velázquez, who lost everything in a rescue attempt, and recovers her faith in humanity after a donation of shoes.

Daisy Day, who finds peace twenty years after her boyfriend was murdered.

And Abby Fisher, one-time accountant, who finds herself in an impossible situation.

So, I present to you, five genre-spanning original stories about heroes. Common or garden variety heroes.

Alexandria Blaelock
Melbourne, Australia
May, 2021

CRACKING THE CODE

It was what passed for morning on a day when you've been forced to take some of your annual leave.

That is to say, about lunchtime, but I had no idea what day it was, and there were no cues like garbage trucks, Australia Post guys on motorbikes, or flocks of brightly coloured school children walking down the street.

I did know that I didn't want to be on "vacation."

I hadn't taken one for years, so despite my protestations about how essential I was, they gave me a three-month sentence.

No excuses. Hand over your laptop and don't even think about contacting anyone at the office.

There was nowhere to go, and nothing to do, and I stayed up late watching the shopping channel and blockbusters made during the war and shortly after, and falling asleep on the couch.

It had been two weeks, and already the house looked like a bomb had gone off.

Not sure what it is about holidays that makes you use every single mug and plate and dish in the house before you wash the dishes.

There's a similar equation for the inner layers of your clothing, but not so much for the outer. I'd worn the same track pants and faded fleece since that first weekend.

And I couldn't have said for sure whether I'd combed my hair or not.

I was pretty sure it had been at least a week since I last showered.

I don't want to know what the mail guy who dropped off the package thought as I stood bleary-eyed and blinking in the daylight to sign for it.

Unemployed layabout at worst, at Death's door somewhere in the middle, or working shifts at best.

Or, in a way that was indefinably worse, not even worth thinking about.

The package sat in the middle of my table, half-hidden by layers of used tissues, junk mail, takeout chopsticks and napkins.

I think there might have been a pair of shoes on there too, and that ought to have made me feel bad because shoes on the table are supposed to be bad luck.

Not that I'm superstitious in general.

And I can't imagine how my luck might get much worse.

Touch wood.

The table is at least wood. Not very good quality, and not very attractive, but certainly wood. It's dented and scarred through living with me for twenty years.

The first dent came when I dropped a wine bottle on it; thankfully full so it didn't break.

I didn't have to open it; I knew exactly what was inside it. I'd found it on the train last Summer. Worn out from scans and a cancer follow-up clinic at the hospital.

It was a nicely laminated hardback notebook, with the cover of a lurid romance - all bright blue sky, blond woman with heaving bosoms clenched to the bare muscular chest of Mr Tall, Dark and Handsome.

The kind of old fashioned romance where he punishes her with a kiss on page 16 and spends the next hundred pages relentlessly bullying her into marriage.

And for some reason, she says yes, perhaps because he gaslighted her into thinking she couldn't do any better.

Along with the book, there should be a myki ticket, a fifty dollar note, and a few store receipts.

I'd dropped it off at the police station about six months before, hoping the detectives could find the writer of the journal it contained.

It had been written by a young woman, whose boyfriend might have gone through abusive and out the other side to potentially life-threatening.

A lot like the romance the notebook's cover evoked.

Or it might have been a fake.

Six months was plenty of time to investigate, so it seemed safe to assume they hadn't found anything, because they sent the book back to me and its owner clearly didn't walk out with it.

I made coffee and took it out to the deck to drink.

The trees stirred in a light breeze and spattered loose raindrops onto the deck. There was no sign of the restless flocks of parrots that roost in the ones behind my house.

Oscar, the cat who'd adopted me at the old place, sauntered out behind me tail in the air and played nonchalantly with leaves blown in by the wind.

He at least seemed to appreciate the extra time I was spending at home.

The air was cold against my face and neck, so I pulled the hood of my fleece up. The cold was invigorating, though it made the inside of my house too warm by contrast.

I wondered if I'd overridden the central heating again.

I would not survive another eleven weeks of this if I didn't do something.

"Uh, Miz Jones?"

I whipped around to see a man leaning through the garden gate trying to get my attention, and I had the sense he'd been calling me for some time.

He was about my age, which is not as old as my white hair would suggest, (the unhappy consequence of my hair falling out during the first attempt at a cancer treatment).

Unlike me, he was dressed in jeans and a polo shirt that looked to be clean, and he glowed with youth and vitality. Which annoyed me about as much as being caught *déshabille* in my own backyard, and I went a bit feral.

"What do you want? What are you doing in my yard?"

Which seemed to amuse him, as if he'd heard stories about the monster, finally met her, and she was everything he'd imagined.

Now that he had my attention, he felt comfortable opening the gate and walking up to the edge of the deck.

"My grandfather tends your yard, I'm here today in his place."

That changed things a bit.

I moved closer to the edge.

"What happened? Is Frank okay?"

The boy grinned at me, "It's just a sprain, he slipped in the bathroom. He'll be fine."

"That's a relief. I take it Alda is taking good care of him?"

He laughed, "he wanted to come here to supervise to get away from her."

I smiled.

To be honest I felt a little jealous.

When I was recovering from the cancer treatment, I had been alone.

Though at the same time, I'd wanted it that way. I can't stand it when people fuss.

Frank had stopped by more frequently than he ought to bring me soup and tiny meatballs, and those little biscuits with jam in them.

And then I realised; the last time Frank had been here, he'd talked a lot about his newly single grandson...

And I might have mentioned my upcoming leave, and possibly the long and completely unscheduled days ahead of me...

All alone.

Abruptly, I became aware that I hadn't spoken to anyone in days and the idea of going back into that house on my own was weirdly horrifying.

"Are you Jed?"

He leaned an elbow against the stair rail, "yeah, how did you know that?"

I snorted, and not in a cute way.

"Any reason you can think of that he asked his computer engineer grandson to take care of my garden rather than, say, his construction grandson?"

"Oh, they've all got other things to do."

"The curse of the freelancer do you think?"

He shrugged, "I don't have any urgent deadlines."

I was pretty sure Frank had not met with any bathroom misfortune.

It was way more likely this was just his sledgehammer subtle way of matchmaking.

But.

He'd caught me in a weak moment.

"Would you like to come in for some coffee?"

Jed looked at me and rearranged his body against the stair rail.

I think he'd just figured out he was the honey trap.

Or I was.

Hard to tell when other people are doing the matchmaking.

"Ahh. Maybe I should just get on with the gardening."

I shrugged a shoulder and let the hand with my empty coffee cup drop, "suit yourself," and walked back inside.

At which point I realised how lucky an escape that was, given the state of the house.

And when I thought about it, me.

Not going to work ought not to be such a drama.

Putting Jed out of my mind, I took a shower and washed my hair.

I hesitated about whether to dress up or down, and eventually went for jeans, and a black button-down shirt. I rolled the sleeves up to pretend I was going to do some work of one kind or another.

And then I tidied and vacuumed, and when I opened the door to take the rubbish out, I ran into Jed just as he was about to knock on the door.

"Oh, the money!" I said, "hold on and I'll get it."

I dropped the rubbish bag on the floor and turned away.

"I'm sorry if I offended you before."

I paused, with my back turned, "no, not to worry. Frank said you'd just broken up with your girl-friend—."

Oops.

Open mouth A, insert foot B.

I looked up to the ceiling for a moment, trying to think of what to say or do, and ended up pretending that last comment hadn't happened.

"Wait here and I'll get your money."

I took a step, but he leaned through the door to grab my arm and stop me from walking away, "no. I mean..."

He dropped my arm, "is your offer of coffee still on?"

"Oh," I said, tucking a stray lock of hair behind my ear, "um," then "ah."

Way to go Gemma. So smooth.

At least I'd tidied up in the meantime.

"Let me just," I turned back to see him depositing the bag in the bin.

"Sure. Come in," I said to his back, but I left the door open as I walked back down the hall.

Lord knows what I was thinking.

That I was lonely.

That he was another human.

Who perhaps thought he had a female body to cry against.

And when I got back to the kitchen, I saw the package from the police service on the table.

Addressed to Miss Gemma Jones.

I hate it when my mail is addressed to my full name.

I picked it up.

The young woman who wrote the journal was obviously weighing on my mind.

And I had eleven weeks on uncommitted time, I could make an effort to find her.

Though did she want to be found?

Perhaps if I plotted out the places she mentioned, I might find a pattern in her movements.

It doesn't really matter how private you expect your journal to be, bits and pieces of identifiable fact slip through. Especially when you use it to manage your business.

Like maybe client names, fragments of copy or design.

"Nice place you have here."

I had forgotten about Jed.

How embarrassing.

I dropped the package back on the table, tucked my hair back behind my ear and moved through to the kitchen area to put the coffee machine on.

He picked it up, and gave me an eye, "what's the statute of limitations on Miss?"

"That's one of those things I hate about being an Anglo. If I lived almost anywhere else, I'd be promoted to Madam by now."

He grinned.

And then it occurred to me, I needed a team.

On those private investigator shows, there's always a computer guy. You can tell he's the computer guy because he (or she) is always wearing glasses and looks like he (or she) couldn't run one hundred metres if his (or her) bus was pulling away from the kerb.

I took a gamble.

"If you had to find someone when you didn't know their name, how would you do that?"

"Well, first, I'm not that kind of engineer, and second, what other information do you have?"

I pulled a chair from the long edge of the table out and gestured for him to sit in it. Then I opened the package and gave him the journal.

He flicked through it while I explained, "I found this journal on the train and handed it in to the police, but I'm guessing they haven't found the writer."

The coffee machine gurgled its last, so I made two mugs. "Milk and sugar?"

"Hmm? Oh. Yes, and no."

I made the changes and put the mug on the table in front of him before taking my usual seat at the head of the table.

And tucking my hair behind my ear again

He took a sip of his coffee, "well, the first thing would be to put your scruples aside and read it carefully for clues."

I rolled my eyes, "what are you? Like twelve?"

He put the book down, pulled himself to his full height, and rested his folded hands on it. "I'll have you know I read every one of the Hardy Boys adventures, and Nancy Drew as well. I know a clue when I find one."

I struggled to keep a straight face, but a smile leaked out nonetheless.

He held the book by the spine, and shook it, then investigated the pocket at the back to discover the myki, cash, and receipts.

He pushed the myki aside, "there's no point tracing that because if she was looking for a new start, she'd move somewhere far away from where she'd lived previously."

I smiled a little; after a quick flick through he'd reached the same conclusion as me; that the writer was female.

"Are you sure, she might have family nearby?"

"Okay, what would you do in that situation?"

I thought about it for a bit.

"I will concede I'd move away, maybe interstate, but I don't have any ties to bind me."

He frowned, "well, if she's gone interstate that'll make it harder to trace her.

"What about the cat?"

"The cat?"

He put his coffee down and swivelled in his seat to look at me, "this cat," and he pointed down at Oscar who was purring and rubbing his face on Jed's jeans.

"Ah. That cat. I'd take him with me."

Jed leaned down and scratched Oscar under the chin.

I guess he'd made his point.

"Why don't you read through the journal again, and I'll search for the stuff?"

I know I'd been thinking of him as "my" computer guy, but I hadn't imagined him wanting to get involved. And even if I did, I hadn't expected him to start right away.

Which led to the awful confession, "I don't have a home computer."

"No problem, laptop's fine."

I had a sense of where this conversation was going, "I don't have one of those either."

He stopped, stunned into motionless, "you don't have any kind of computer at home?"

"Well, there's an ancient tablet I use for ebooks, but it's been ages since I had a computer that wasn't owned by my employer."

"No wonder you're going nuts here on your—"

Perhaps the conversation between him and his grandfather hadn't been exactly the matchmaking one I'd been thinking it was.

That Frank thought I was going a bit nuts felt like a betrayal.

I turned my back towards Jed, only there was nowhere to go; it was *my* house, and walking away defeated the purpose.

This was exactly why I don't have a lot of friends, and don't invite them in. Once they're here, they leave thought and memory traces that can't be eradicated.

But I started walking in the direction of the front door, and when I got there, I opened it, stepped out and just kept walking.

He caught up with me halfway down the street and fell into step.

"Look, I'm sorry. I didn't mean to hurt your feelings; the words just slipped out. Frank's worried about you."

"I don't need your pity. Or his. I'm fine on my own."

My eyes were watering, and it was taking too much energy to hold them in.

I'd blame it on the drugs, only I was transitioning out of them.

I stopped walking and couldn't prevent myself from leaning towards him. He didn't move away.

Not matchmaking, I reminded myself, babysitting.

I straightened up and started walking back towards my house. If he couldn't catch me, I'd lock him outside.

And of course he could catch me.

"Ok, so maybe you don't need or want my help.

"You can go down to just about any electronics, computer or department store and for about a grand you can get a reasonable laptop with a good battery life, a display good enough for games or streaming, and a fairly good-size memory.

"I'll leave it with you."

And rather than follow me into the house, he watched me walk through the door and shut it.

I heard his car drive away.

And ridiculously, almost immediately wanted him to come back.

And then I told myself to get a grip on myself and sat down with the notebook, and my own journal to make notes.

I tucked my hair behind my ear.

First, I reviewed the store receipts. Stationery, storage boxes, lunch. Were they expense receipts? Were they from her old place or her new? I started a new page in my journal and noted the dates and locations.

And then I remembered I had an old Melways map book, so I started mapping them out to see if some kind of pattern might show itself.

I skipped over the contents, long-term to-dos and miscellaneous list pages of the book, and went straight to the calendars.

The monthly and weekly calendars were marked with stickers folded around the edges of the pages, so I flicked through to the first and checked the dates looking for appointments, deadlines, and to-dos, and where possible the locations.

The first month noted hair and a doctor's appointment. And as I flicked through the following months, a grant application deadline, a half-day seminar, an online workshop, a short story deadline, and so on until I had a reasonable list of dates that might lead to some viable next steps.

Then I skimmed through the daily pages in between, and these included meeting notes, voice mail transcriptions, and the girl working through issues that bothered her. That yielded even more clues for my notebook.

I snorted recalling Jed's self-righteous defence of his amateur detective skills.

Though I guess I had to give him credit for coming up with the same search parameters as me.

And then it occurred to me, that the diary might record information that could identify the violent boyfriend, so I skimmed through it again to make a note of those details.

By that point, it was clear to me she was a virtual assistant, so from that point of view, she could relocate anywhere in Australia. Though the fact that she seemed to specialise in an Australian context didn't mean she couldn't work anywhere else.

While I thought about what I'd learned, I changed back in to track pants and an oversize fleece, (clean this time), and as my hair had been giving me the shits all day, pulled it back into a ponytail.

Thinking I should really get it cut.

I wasn't real keen to get messed up again any time soon, so I cleared up the mess I'd made with Jed, emptied the dishwasher and put the two mugs inside.

Was it only that morning?

As I tossed the envelope the book came in across the kitchen to the recycling bin, something fell out of it.

It was a short note, indicating the detectives had not found any evidence of foul play, and therefore the case had been closed, and the book returned to me.

Well, of course they hadn't found any evidence - the journal didn't record any serious injuries. Not to mention that it ended before any serious assaults occurred. But if you read between the lines, she'd been terrified by the time it ended.

Clearly, Police Officers require a higher evidentiary standard than I do, but did they even look?

Or was that perhaps why the Police Officer I'd handed it to had given it back? Though with her impressively impassive face, she hadn't seemed unduly concerned at the time.

Had things changed? Had she been less than satisfied by her male colleagues' treatment of the matter?

And as he'd been involved, I wanted to test the idea on Jed.

Basically, because there was no one else.

It was a good excuse to call him, though somewhat less of a good excuse to call Frank and ask for his number.

Especially given that whole going a bit nuts thing.

The sky was darkening by this point, and I judged it was a reasonable hour to take a glass of wine or two before considering what takeout to order for tea.

And then it occurred to me that I was still going to the hairdresser I used to go to when I lived in the old place.

The one that took me two trains and an hour to get there, and two trains and a bus to get back. That I continued to take a day off every time I visited because the idea of having to explain my hair to someone else was exhausting.

I went back to her journal, and checked the dates - it spanned about four months. I checked my list of dates and appointments, and there were two hair appointments at the same place.

And it looked as though she might be about due another.

Could it really be that simple?

The main problem being, that I relied on public transport, and didn't own a car. I suppose I could hire one, but it'd been a long time since I'd driven anywhere.

Did I dare ask Jed?

All rightie, I'll admit it. I was starting to obsess just a little bit about Jed. He was kinda handsome in a tanned, dark-haired way, and he had a kinda confident, easy-going way about him.

But it was probably the drugs, because transitioning out of them substituted one set of issues for another.

At least until they're out of your system altogether.

So, yeah.

Probably the drugs.

I opened a nice bottle of Cabernet Sauvignon and left it to breathe while I got a glass and some Roquefort and crackers to eat with it.

And my phone so I could check the app to work out the best way to get to the hairdresser.

At which point, the doorbell rang.

It was Jed.

"Ah. I'm sorry to bother you again."

"Just come in, there's a lot to discuss."

He opened his mouth, then shut it again.

I left the door open and walked down to the kitchen to get another glass.

He shut the door and followed me down, depositing a laptop on the table.

"I felt bad about the computer thing, so I brought this old one of mine you can use."

I snorted as I filled the glass and handed it to him.

"Cheers," I said as I sat in my usual seat.

He echoed me and took the one he'd used before.

"I think I've worked it out."

He raised an eyebrow at me, and I laid my hand on the book.

"And your conclusion?"

"She used the same hairdresser twice in the book, and if that's a repeatable pattern, might be due another appointment."

"Ah, of course. What do you want to do now?"

I took a sip of wine, "I think I have to visit the salon to see if they know who she is."

"Where is it?"

"Heidelberg."

He took a sip of wine and looked at me for a bit. "Want me to take you?"

I couldn't help but smile, "would you?"

And he smiled back, "I surely would."

The next day, he arrived about eight in the morning, and we drove out to the hair salon, timing it for a little later than her appointment might start.

He waited outside while I went inside.

"This is a bit of an odd request, and you don't have to tell me, but can you look up who had an appointment at 9am on September 10, and again at 9am on November 5th last year?"

The woman behind the computer looked at me oddly, but looked the appointments up, and said, "the same woman for both."

"Okay good. Can you look and tell me if she has another one soon?"

She gave me a hard look, and said, "yes."

"Right. That's good too. I have something of hers, and I'd like to give it back."

She looked over my shoulder, and I wondered if she was looking at someone in particular, or was searching her memory for something.

"There's a coffee shop around the corner, why don't you go get a coffee and I'll call her."

I smiled, "thanks, that would be wonderful. It's her journal."

She nodded, and I turned away, resolutely not looking at any of the women in the salon.

"Do you want me to come with you?" Jed asked.

"Maybe in the same place, but not at the same table?"

"Good idea."

We ordered coffees, and while I waited, I got out my journal and wrote about what was happening.

It wasn't long before a youngish blonde woman with foils folded up in her hair, and a hair salon cape around her shoulders came in.

She clearly knew who she was looking for, as she approached me and sat down without hesitation.

"You have something for me?"

All very cloak and dagger.

"Why don't you tell me what you think it is, and I'll tell you if you're right?"

"It's a hard-covered journal with an old romance cover picture on it."

And that seemed enough, so I took it out of my bag and put it on the table.

She looked at it for a while.

"Are you okay?" I asked.

"You made me realise how easy it is to find me."

"Can't be that easy, the Police didn't find you."

She sighed, "I've changed everything else, but I couldn't let go of my hairdresser. It's such an easy tell."

"Only for those who know who she is."

"Well, if you, a total stranger found me, it would be a cinch for someone who knows me better."

"I hope you find someone kinder, and more respectful."

Her eyes brimmed with tears, and I had no idea what to do or say to make her feel better.

"I should go. I hope we don't meet again," and she took the journal and left the cafe.

Jed picked up his coffee and came across to my table.

"I think we made it worse."

He patted my hand. "Better to know now than to think she was safe until her ex turned up."

I sighed, "then why don't I feel better about this?"

"You should be proud of yourself. You solved a mystery and gave the girl fair warning."

I looked at his stupid smiling face.

But I *had* done that.

In the ugliest possible way, I had made her safer.

THE END

NEVER GOING TO BE A HERO

If Veronica was on a planet, she'd be in one of those odd job kiosks at the bottom of the train station or parking structure. The kind of kiosk you can drop off your dry cleaning, appliances to be fixed, keys to be cut in the morning and pick them up in the evening.

The kind of kiosk that's so filthy with decades of train and parking dust and grime you wonder whether you'll need a tetanus shot to just walk past it.

And smells like generations of men have relieved themselves on the side of it.

That's almost obscured by cardboard sheets of key rings, carabiners and penknives you don't want to touch with a barge pole, that don't seem to sell, and have been there so long they've curled inward at the edges.

That never seems to have any business, yet never shuts down, and makes you wonder if it just exists to launder drug money.

But Veronica, also known as Vee, lives on Mephisto station, and they don't have basements.

At one end of the scale, you can get a large luxury apartment in the core, with plant supplemented oxygen, simulated sunlight, barely recycled water and oxygen, and reliable gravity.

Well, you can, if you can afford it...

Or if, like Vee, you want something cheap, you'll find it on the edge where the gravity is less than reliable, oxygen not as well-scrubbed, and if there's a meteor strike or someone crash-lands you might lose your home.

Technically, units on the edge are zoned for industrial and commercial purposes only, with communal kitchens and washrooms set at intervals around the rim. But that's where Vee, and the poorest of the poor live.

Not because she's destitute, but because she doesn't want to attract attention.

She's going straight now.

And she feels like she owes it to humanity to make amends.

Vee's unit, like all the others, was an empty, more or less rectangular room measuring twenty-four square metres, with a safety glass frontage so people can see what you're selling.

The light from the main corridors forms a useful supplement to the three strip lights inside.

The lights are controlled by one light switch, and the empty unit also contained two power sockets, one air outlet and one communications hub access point.

She installed a counter at the front, shelves and workbenches in the middle, and a tiny area behind the last shelving unit to sleep in.

And added one air freshener approximating the smell of lavender, rosemary and fresh air to counter-act the smell of boiled cabbage coming from the air outlet.

And may have illegally jury-rigged the power outlets.

Vee buys, sells and repairs small electronics, so the shelves are crammed with bits and pieces of housing, wires, transistors, capacitors, diodes, bits of circuit board, switches, connectors and other useful things.

The inners throw out a lot of stuff when it stops working, so their day workers (who live in the outer), fish it out of the bins and sell it to Vee to supplement their meagre wages. At least, that's what they do when they don't get caught.

Vee breaks them into components and uses them to repair the toasters and rice cookers the outers rely on and can't afford to replace.

When the outers do get caught, the inners generally demand the goods back so they can throw them out properly. Then they sack the outers (as they are easily replaceable), and demand penalties that generally amount to several days' wages.

Which is why Vee also scours the garbage dumps for items that might be useful one day.

Sometimes the inner's fancy food doesn't make it to the bin either. Somehow it gets to the black market too.

And because you never know when you might need a favour, it's not uncommon that Vee might be offered a wafer-thin slice of cake on someone's birthday.

She also practises a bit of field dentistry and medicine, when you've been injured and don't want anyone asking too many questions.

Or when you're skint and can't afford a proper doctor, she only charges for the goods and not her time.

That's why she's very popular with the outers, and they'll often call in for a chat. And because she chats, she always knows a fella who can get you what you need.

It was a kind of life that suited Vee well. She was more or less at ease. With people who were more or less friends.

It'd been a few years, and she was just starting to let her guard down...

She was sharing a glass of rotgut with Tim as she picked bits of industrial drill from his leg when he said, "I've heard a rumour Black Eyed Benny's on the station."

She helped herself to another shot, and pored one for him, "isn't there a warrant out for his arrest?"

"He came in via the smuggler's route," meaning someone had shipped him in as cargo, "word is, he's looking for someone."

"Any idea who?" she asked, taking advantage of his out-breath to pull a shard from his leg.

He gasped and knocked his drink back.

"Isn't that more or less your department?"

She grunted, and smoothed her bloodstained hands down his leg, looking for lumps that might indicate other fragments that needed removing.

Tim grunted and poured another round, drinking his almost immediately.

"Haven't heard anything, but if he's here, Ping can't be far behind."

"She's that psycho bitch from the Jade Dragon triad?"

Vee grunted in agreement as she pulled a threaded needle from her kit.

Tim gritted his teeth while she and quickly and neatly stitched the wounds up, and added a layer of non-stick dressing to each wound.

"You're not going to listen if I tell you to take a day off, are you?"

He grinned, "I got a wife and kids to support."

She drank her drink, and grinned as she poured two more, "thought you'd say that. Try to go easy on that leg, and take one of these pills when the pain gets bad, but be warned, it'll knock you out."

She sighed as she handed him two green pills.

There was no point Tim asking for protective equipment when there were others who'd work without it.

And there was no point going to the company doctor because if he did, he'd be out of a job.

"If you can't get a leather apron, wear your thickest pants dunderhead," she punched his shoulder, "they're better than nothing."

He sighed too, and held his drink up to salute her, "thanks Vee."

She clinked it with hers, "your good health."

He stood to leave, "here, take the bottle," she said.

"But your fee—"

"I think you need it more than me, you take it and bring me another some other time."

He nodded and turned away. She walked him out and watched him hobble away.

Then turned in the other direction and went for a bowl of spicy noodles, with whatever they were passing off as meat that day.

There was no point locking the door, if anyone wanted to get in, they would.

But, in general, people were more often asking for favours of her, so it was in their best interests to make sure she and her stuff were all okay.

Also, the good stuff was stored somewhere else, and anyone with a lick of sense would figure that out.

The main thing was to collect data about Ben and Ping, because despite what she'd said to Tim, she knew Ben was looking for her.

He was an old boyfriend who wouldn't take no for an answer, followed by Ping who wanted to be his new girlfriend.

Lucky she'd been a Jade Dragon liaison at the time and knew how to take care of herself.

Not to mention friendly with the Jade Dragon Mountain Master, and having bought out her contract was leaving the organisation on friendly terms.

It was a shame she wasn't permitted to kill Ben as a condition of her unencumbered release.

Though she'd shot him three times to slow him down.

And slipped him twice before, but dammit, she was sick of running.

She liked Mephisto station, there were good people here.

And quite aside from that, she liked the retro-architecture.

She'd made a mistake thinking Ping would keep him out of her hair.

Ping, for her poor deluded part, wanted him to love her, to want to be with her.

She wasn't keen to keep him banged up, and for that matter, his job in the Jade Dragon didn't really allow for that.

Vee'd always had a problem asking others for help, and Ping wasn't much good at doing favours anyway.

As she ate her noodles, people stopped to chat.

Bought her a drink, dropped off bits and pieces they thought might be useful.

She twisted some wires into a small animal, maybe a dog, though neither she nor the child she made it for had ever seen one.

But more importantly, they passed on information.

It seemed Ben was on-station and waving her picture about.

She'd made some small cosmetic changes through a friend of a friend of a Jade Dragon surgeon, so his photo and description wouldn't be much use.

Nor any of the names he was asking for.

If Ping had arrived, she was keeping a low profile.

Potentially, Vee still had some time to make plans.

She forced herself to walk as slowly as if it was an ordinary day and she had all the time in the world.

As if she wasn't worried about anything.

And as she walked, she paused here and there to talk. Laying her hands on people, in celebration, in commiseration, and not that they knew it, but in blessing.

Worrying about what might happen to them and station if she couldn't keep it safe.

When she got back to her room, it seemed nothing had been disturbed.

Only the lingering scent of sandalwood betrayed the fact that someone more fastidious than the usual spacer had been in her shop.

She glanced at the atmosphere monitor she'd altered to detect common poisons and it was clear.

Closing her eyes, and focusing on her other senses, she couldn't hear breathing, the room was still, and remained at one standard unit of gravity.

Aside from the sandalwood, there were no other scents.

She opened her eyes, and looking with more intention, saw the path Sandalwood had taken through the shop where they'd picked up items and set them down inexactly.

The displaced objects suggested a weird kind of tenderness, that only someone familiar with her deep past would have known about. A badly made cup. A charm bracelet. A puzzle box.

If Sandalwood was Ben, it might be enough to trigger his suspicion.

The perfume of sandalwood was stronger as she proceeded through the room to her tiny sleeping space, and there on the bed, was a folded green robe topped with a sword, and a green object about the size of her fist.

At first, she thought it was a plastic ball of something, but when she picked it up, she realised it was carved stone.

Jade.

Smooth on the bottom, but the dragon ridges so sharp on the top she'd cut herself before she realised.

A jade dragon.

She put her hand to her lips and sucked the edge of it.

The green robe signified Justice, the balance between order and chaos.

The jade dragon statue represented the authority to dispense Justice; protecting the deserving and punishing those who go against the Order of the Jade Dragon.

Lastly, the sword, said to have been passed down to the chosen one for hundreds of generations, representing the threat, and in some cases, the action of Justice.

The Mountain Master had summoned her to join the triad tribunal.

Theoretically, she could refuse...

But she wouldn't be putting any odds on herself to survive, because whoever the envoy was, they'd be watching.

Not Ben of course, it would be someone she didn't know.

On the other hand, taking the green robe offered a promotion of a sort. A role outside the triad, dispensing justice when required.

Not exactly in, not exactly out.

Her word as law.

Her only real option was to wait for the summons. She didn't have to wait long.

A couple of days later, one of the station urchins who lived in the walls brought a sandalwood scented envelope. The card within told her when and where to go, and nothing else.

In triad Justice, you didn't know who your judge was, or what the charges were before you got the summons.

On the designated evening she set off with the robe, statue and sword stuffed into a backpack, and a couple of daggers in her boots, and got as close as she could without being detected.

Then she donned the robe, pulling the hood forward to hide her face.

She took a deep breath, letting the vestigial sandalwood scent sit in her lungs for a moment, before breathing out her fear and continuing her journey.

She swept into the warehouse, sword in her left hand, statue in the right.

As she ascended the makeshift podium, the excited voices of the witnesses rose.

As she sat in the large chair in the centre of the podium, placing the dragon on the arm of the chair and holding the sword in both hands in her lap, the voices died away.

She was grateful the sandalwood incense masked the smell of unwashed people.

Three people stepped out from the crowd.

A tall man she hadn't seen before walked toward her, bowed, and outlined the charges.

She assumed he was the Master's envoy.

Essentially, the first guy was encroaching on the territory of the second guy. The first guy was invited to address her, and then the second.

Generally, territory was sacrosanct, though if you didn't fully exploit the rights of the territory, it was open to others who would do so.

Vee raised the sheathed sword to pointed towards the second guy, who smiled and bowed. The first guy took a step forward and started arguing with her.

She pulled the sword a couple of inches from its scabbard, and he fell silent.

"The Justice has spoken," the envoy said, repeating the judgement for all to hear, to record it for the Master, and the central records.

The second case involved the theft of stolen goods. She didn't listen to the arguments they made; chances are they were both liars.

Instead, she watched the body language as they spoke. One seemed more open, and the other closed, so she found in favour of the open.

The third case involved people smuggling. The goods had not arrived in a saleable condition. Too many had died in transit, and the cost of saving those who had arrived was too much.

Vee didn't even bother listening to the arguments, just tapped the tip of the sheathed sword on the floor, and beckoned the envoy to approach.

He knelt before her.

"Confiscate the goods to my control," she said.

He looked up under her hood, searching what he could see of her face, and after a pause, nodded.

Declaring the result, and the end of the day's proceedings.

Vee waited for a moment, then picked up the statue in her right hand, and walked out, once again carrying the sword in her left.

This was where it would get tricky; in the robe, with the sword, she was obvious, and needed to get far enough away to disrobe and stuff the gear into the backpack without anyone noticing her.

And then get back to the shop so she could hide it without anyone noticing anything suspicious.

Luck, and her deep familiarity with the station was on her side.

She sat at her workstation, surrounded by bits and bobs of wires, and heaved a sigh of relief.

Of course, if she had to regularly dispense Justice, she wouldn't be able to keep her Jade Dragon connection a secret.

Though she wasn't entirely sure she'd managed this time.

But for the moment, she'd take a drink and let her heart rate settle.

She heard the door open, and then she heard a snick as the bolt shot home.

She tensed, ready to reach for the daggers still in her boots.

And then she caught a scent she'd almost forgotten; bergamot, patchouli and musk.

Ben.

On top of everything else.

How tiresome.

"I found you," he said in a sing-song voice, and she couldn't help but roll her eyes.

How could he be the same when she had changed so much?

"What do you want?"

He laughed, "I want you of course!"

"Well, I don't want you. How many times do I have to tell you?"

Not for the first time she thought wistfully of applying one, or both, of the daggers in her boots to assorted soft tissues in his body.

All she needed now, was Ping to turn up.

And almost as soon as she'd formed the thought, the safety glass door shattered, and Ping stepped through the pieces.

As if the day couldn't get any worse.

Ping launched into a verbal offensive, mainly directed at Ben.

Vee didn't bother listening, she'd heard it twice before, she focused on quickly and silently withdrawing, hopefully before either of them realised what she was up to.

As she reached the counter, she noticed the envoy leaning on a wall a couple of shops down, paring his fingernails with a knife.

He gave her no indication he'd seen her, but the swift, sure movements of the knife gave her an idea.

As a Justice of the triad, her word was law; she could put an official end to this.

She wondered if she dared.

Turning around, she saw Ping had bailed Ben up against a shelving unit. Sensible of him not to have harmed her, given she was a blood relative of the Master, one who had a shot at becoming the Master herself at some point.

They clearly had an easy familiarity with each other's bodies.

"I just don't understand what you see in her," Ping said, looking up at him with tears glistening between her eyelashes.

Vee rolled her eyes.

"Why is it her, and not me?" Ping continued.

Vee made retching noises, and they turned to look at her as if they'd forgotten her.

"Really?" she said, "really?"

She leant on the counter and pointed at Ping.

"You are a criminal mastermind. You basically run half the galaxy, and all you really care about what he does and where he goes?"

She turned to point at Ben, "despite everything, you almost always end going back to Ping. Why do you have to annoy me and everyone in the galaxy with this nonsense?"

Ping glared at her, "how dare you interfere in Jade Dragon business, you should leave before I get annoyed and kill you."

"You can't kill her," Ben said, "I'll kill you before you get to her."

"I'd rather be dead than listen to this crap for a minute longer," Vee said, and put the Jade Dragon and sword on the counter.

Ben gasped, and Ping stepped away from him.

"Right," said Vee, "Ben, give me your best shot."

Ben spluttered, but paused too long.

"Ping?"

Likewise, Ping was caught out.

"Well then, this is my Justice." She walked across to Ben, and pushed him to the ground.

"Ben, you will be contracted to Ping for one Earth standard year. You may not leave her side unless she tells you to.

"Ping, when the year is up, you must let him go. Whether he chooses to stay with you or not is up to him.

"Further, Justices must remain independent, and apart, so neither of you may approach me again.

"Ping, take this useless piece of shit, and get the hell off my station."

Ping laughed, "you have no one to record your judgement, so it's not binding."

"On the contrary," the envoy's voice said from behind Vee, "the Justice has spoken, and her word is the law."

"Come on Ping," Ben said, "Justice is delivered, let's get out of here."

He took her wrist and led her from the shop.

"Gutsy move," the envoy said.

"'Spose. I just wanted them gone."

"Drink?"

"God yes."

He pulled a small, ornate bottle of something from his pocket and put it on the counter.

She put the sword and dragon back in her pack and stowed it in a small nook concealed behind the sleeping chamber, and returned with two glasses.

He poured the alcohol and raised his glass to her.

She chinked it with her own and sipped the drink. "So, what's next?"

"Well, you need to make arrangements for 16 smuggled people."

Vee laughed, "I'd forgotten about them."

"Well, they'll be here soon, so you'd better start thinking about it."

"Hmmm," she said, rubbing her eyes with the heels of her hands. Right at that moment, it was too hard to figure out where she'd get papers and where to put them.

"But, you did a good job," the envoy said, "the Master will be pleased."

She sighed, "I never wanted to be a hero, but out on my own, I'd hoped I could help people."

"You were never going to be a hero; your skills aren't the kind heroes are made of. You're the kind of person who gets things up and running again after the heroes have trashed the place and moved on."

She snorted, "making a difference in my own way."

"I'll drink to that."

THE END

ALL IN

Rosa Velázquez forced herself up the last five steps, and believing the sound wouldn't travel through the solid door at the top, stood panting on the red brick landing.

Her thighs ached, and her feet screamed in agony.

God, she was out of shape.

Would she ever be that fit again? With her feet that scarred, it didn't seem likely.

The door was plain, stained a rich jarrah red, with an old-fashioned black steel lever handle.

And a tiny, handwritten tag in a black steel frame beside the door; Jude Webb, Bespoke Shoes.

He was supposed to be the best in Melbourne.

Which was why she'd climbed three flights of stairs to his Hardware Lane workshop.

Despite her misgivings about the anonymous donation of his services.

Quite frankly she was suspicious of both of him and her benefactor. Always assuming they were, in fact, different people.

But her feet hurt with every step she took, and the lure of handmade shoes, with extra cushioning in the sole was too tempting to stand on her principles and refuse.

She tapped on the door.

No sound of acknowledgement came from within.

She thumped it as hard as she could.

Still nothing.

Admittedly, her thumping barely made much more noise than her tapping.

She pulled the handle down, leaned into it with her shoulder, and overbalanced as it turned out to be ridiculously easy to move.

"I'll just be a moment," he said, his back turned to her, "please take off your shoes and take a seat on the chair."

The man inside was much younger than she'd expected for a Master craftsman.

With his thick dark hair, she'd say early thirties.

He was wearing a thick, white cotton shirt with the sleeves rolled up, and a blue tweed vest with matching trousers.

He looked like he belonged in a different century.

She looked at him doubtfully, seemingly engrossed in shaving the leather from the sole of one shoe with a sharp and slender bladed knife. One tanned finger testing the edge of the cuts.

A lock of his shoulder-length hair fell from where he'd tucked it behind his ear, brushing his collar. Was that the corner of some kind of tattoo peeking out from behind the collar?

She stepped up on the platform and took her shoes off, placing them neatly side by side next to the chair, and her bag next to them.

She clasped her scarred hands between her skinny jean-clad thighs and looked around the room.

The red wooden workbench was placed under the crittal windows.

Their black steel frames were a nice contrast against the red brick of the exposed walls, the red wood of the exposed beams, and the white ceiling liner that reflected the dim winter light around the room.

Jude sat at one end of the bench, on a matching adjustable stool with three legs, a small lamp shedding extra light on his work. A combination of hand and handheld power tools were neatly arranged in racks under the windows.

At the other end of the bench, there was a small laptop, connected to an electronic payment machine and a small printer.

A couple of speakers, also connected by wires, sat on the edges of the pillars that supported the ceiling joists. Quietly playing some kind of Latin dance music.

Jarrah racks with blank pine lasts seemingly arranged at random lined one wall, a second held racks of fragrant leather, and the last supported large machinery of some kind.

Rosa snuck a look at Jude's shoes.

Highly polished black leather, elasticated sides, almond-shaped toe, Cuban heel.

Nice pair of Chelsea boots.

She had almost the same pair back home, though off the rack, not made to measure.

Not leather, and not comfortable either.

Not that she could bear to wear them anymore. It was probably time to throw out all her shoes.

Jude swivelled on the seat to look at her, wiping his hands on a grey apron she hadn't noticed until then.

He took it off and hung it on a peg by the bench.

"Sorry about that," he said, walking towards her holding out his callused hand, "I'm Jude Webb."

She stood to take it, "Rosa Velázquez." His hand was warm and strong, almost completely enveloping her own.

"Can you roll up your jeans?"

She looked at her legs, "I'm afraid not."

A smile crossed his face so quickly she wasn't sure she'd seen it.

"I need to see and assess the condition of your ankles. Would you be comfortable taking them off and wearing a blanket instead?"

She looked uneasily down at her legs. He couldn't see it, but the scarring was severe.

"Or perhaps you'd like to come another day?"

She squared her shoulders; she hadn't walked up all those stairs just to walk straight back down them with nothing to show for the effort.

"No, it's okay. Give me the blanket."

He handed her the blanket, and she clutched it to her chest, "I'll wait outside, let me know when you're ready."

《《 • 》》

Jude shut the door and leaned his back against it. Almost as if he had a wild creature trapped inside the workshop and didn't want to let it out.

Which in a way, he did.

Rosa Velázquez was like a ray of light shining into his workshop. Outshining the dim winter light leaking through the windows of his art deco workshop.

Though in the day's defence, it was cloudy and midwinter; it could barely compete against the fluorescent lighting let alone Rosa Velázquez.

Her name had seemed familiar when the appointment came in, so he'd looked her up on the internet.

Two years ago, Rosa Velázquez, a secretary waiting for the bus on her way to work, had run *into* a burning building and saved the life of a mother, then *gone back in* to save her two children.

She'd been lucky, clearing the house with the last child in her arms, just moments before it collapsed.

Somewhat less lucky, she'd been wearing a polyester suit and synthetic leather shoes, which had melted into her skin in addition to the burns from the fire.

Rosa was literally a hero. A bona fide hero with several medals to prove it.

Rosa startled him by opening the door a crack.

Her hair was cropped close to her head, and her serious, impossibly blue eyes showed a mixture of fear and stubbornness.

"You can come in now."

He tucked his hair behind his ear again and grinned at her, the light blanket folded over her blouse and around her body like a sarong.

He leaned on the door, and as she backed up, gestured for her to precede him.

She sat on the chair again, and he knelt before her.

"I understand you're looking for oxfords?"

She cleared her throat, "I was until I say your boots."

"Okay," he grinned as he saw her looking again, "why don't you tell me exactly what you're looking for?"

He looked up at her as she started talking, marvelling at her delicate facial features as she talked about how much pain she felt walking, and how she wanted beautiful shoes because she was sick of wearing clumpy ugly shoes, and how her feet weren't as flexible as they had been, and she worried she'd never walk properly again.

There was not one word that stuck inside his head, but he was beginning to form an idea of the shoes he was planning to make her.

"Would you be wearing socks or stockings with these shoes?"

"Um, I have some compression socks."

He grunted.

First, he picked up her shoes and examined them inside and out to see where the wear was, and how she was carrying her weight.

"May I?" he said, gesturing at her feet.

She nodded, and he picked up her left foot, rubbing and bending it to see its formation, checking for calluses as well as heel and toe deformities.

Aside from the obvious scars.

Jude started moving up her leg, under the blanket, and she gasped and stiffened.

He stopped immediately, "I need to check your ankles too."

After a moment she relaxed, and he continued, testing the thickness of her ankle, and the thinness of her bones.

And maybe he went a tiny bit further up her calve than he needed to, but the scarring was misleading.

"Did anyone talk to you about scar massage?"

"No, not really."

He frowned, "then this might hurt a bit," he moved her ankle from side to side, and bent more firmly on her feet.

She held it as long as she could, and then squeaked in protest.

"I'm sorry," he said, then started again with her right foot.

"About the compression socks?" he said putting her foot back on the floor.

She leaned across to her bag, pulled them out and handed them to him.

He put his hand in the sock and stretched it out, "good, just a little light compression at this point."

"How is that good?"

"Ordinary socks just hold your foot in place, these ones have a little compression around the arches, which means the shoes don't have to do as much work."

"Ah."

He grinned, "it also means the shoe can be a little more relaxed, and maybe, I could do a low-heeled Mary Jane, or even a Chelsea Boot."

The hope in her eyes was heartbreaking.

"Why did you ask about scar massage?"

"Do your scars still itch?"

"A bit?"

"Massaging the scars can help reduce the itching, and relax the scars, making them more flexible. Would you like me to show you?"

She nodded.

"Okay, let me finish up measuring first."

He pulled the socks onto her feet with practised ease, and drew around her feet, noting the measurement of the widest part of her feet, the middle of the arch, where the foot and leg meet, and the length of her heel.

"I'll be right back," he said, shoving his papers aside, and ducked out of the room.

《《 • 》》

Rosa was surprised by how gentle his hands were.

And how he looked at her like she was the centre of the universe.

She liked it.

And she liked the way his hazel eyes deepened to a chocolate colour when he looked up at her for longer than a glance.

She was so used to the sight of her scars being all people could see, that it had taken her a moment to notice that he didn't seem to see the scars. He looked through them to see her.

In fact, her ex-boyfriend hadn't even been able to look at her after the fire and had moved out of their apartment while she was still in the hospital.

She really could have done with his support, and hadn't realised he was so shallow.

Pride kept her from phoning him.

But at that moment, she could see an end to her loneliness.

That the scars might not matter to someone else.

If she gave someone the chance, they might want to get to know her better.

Maybe that someone could be Jude Webb; he might want to date her.

And maybe touch a little more than just her feet and legs.

She'd like that too.

Was she brave enough to ask him out for a drink?

Not just a latte in the cafe on the ground floor of his building, but a proper drink in the fashionable bar further down the laneway.

Maybe some dinner.

She stretched her arms and legs out in front of her, imagining a more intimate end to the evening.

But the scars pulled her up with a sharp pain, reminding her what she'd lost.

Wishful thinking couldn't change the fact of her condition.

She decided to cut and run. It seemed he had everything he needed, she could send him an email to apologise later.

She was halfway back into her jeans, getting ready to take off when he walked through the door holding a jar of cream.

"Sorry to take so long, I had to—," his voice and steps trailing to a standstill.

Rosa clutched at the blanket to hide herself, and tried to say something, "I..."

She realised she didn't have the words to describe what she was feeling, so she turned away.

He dropped the cream, and in three large steps had crossed the workroom, circled her with his arms, and drew her back against his chest, "I understand."

All the pain and frustration she'd felt since the fire consumed her, and she sobbed; harsh guttural convulsions.

Her legs lost all their strength and she would have fallen if he hadn't caught her and gently lowered her to the floor.

As it was, she folded herself around her knees, not really aware he'd tucked between his legs. He cradled her with one arm, and patted her back with the other, one strong pat following a second or two after the one before.

It was calming, and after a time, she stopped crying.

"I'm sorry," she said, not game to raise her head.

He didn't stop patting, "you've been through a lot, I expect it comes out when you least expect it."

She snorted, then sniffed, then reached for her bag for a tissue.

A clean white handkerchief, smelling of laundry soap, sunshine and lavender was pressed into her hand.

"Thank you," she said, and blew her nose three times until it was clear.

Still looking at the floor, and not at him, "does this happen to you all the time?"

"No. My customers are usually businessmen who think they're more special than they are."

She sat up, and he let his arm fall away. She looked into his face, almost level with hers and full of compassion.

"Then how do you come to make shoes for people like me?"

"Heroes you mean?"

She flapped her hand in irritation with him, "anyone would have done the same."

"That's not true, you're one in a million. How many people were waiting at the bus stop with you?"

She scrubbed her face with both hands and then went a little further to scratch her head. Drooping in the face of his admiration.

"Being a hero costs more than you might think."

"I know."

"The medals don't mean shit when you lose your job and people turn away in disgust."

"I know."

"How do you know?"

"My mother was in an industrial accident. She found it hard in the beginning, but her counsellor told her that people were afraid it could happen to them. That she was a visual reminder they should enjoy the good times, and the bad times, and cherish one another."

"I like it," she sighed and looked out the window at the cloudy sky. "Cherish. There's not enough cherishing in the world."

"On that subject," he reached for the cream and waggled it at her, "scar massage?"

"I should go."

"There's no should here. No obligations, no duty, no propriety. There are only choices here. The choice to leave, or the choice to stay."

"But your work!"

He laughed, "I'm charging hideous amounts of money to make shoes by hand, and I have a waiting list of months. I think I can spare a few hours with you."

"It's not going to take hours is it?" she asked, horrified at the thought.

"No. You probably won't be able to take much more than a few minutes. But I'd like to do something...

"Oh, I don't know," he shrugged, "nice for you."

She looked into his face again, searching for any trace of sarcasm or disdain, but it was as open and honest as when she'd first walked in.

She dared, once more, to imagine something more. Let her imagination flit between Friday movie nights curled up on the couch with him, and Sunday brunches at local cafes.

If she didn't open herself up, she would never know.

What was the worst that could happen? A couple of hours of fun, and decades of loneliness after.

She had no qualms running into a burning building, and yet she was hesitating about this?

It might not be forever, but it would be one step closer to a normal life. There had to be a first, why not him?

She shrugged and unfolded her legs, lifting one slightly higher than the other "help me with these?"

He pulled the hem of the jeans down and off her leg, and then the other, folding them up and laying them aside before smoothing the blanket across her legs.

Then he shucked off his boots, sat cross-legged before her, and drew her feet into his lap.

He rubbed his hands together, then picked up her left foot.

His hands were hot.

"The best results," he said, dipping his fingers into the cream, "is with little circles to break up the scar."

He demonstrated, "then rubbing up and down the scar," he demonstrated that too.

"And a little pinch and release along the length."

He didn't say anything else as he gently massaged her feet and legs.

It did hurt, but it was a good kind of hurt. The kind that suggested growth.

She couldn't say anything for certain about her scars, but she felt her heart unfreeze a little.

"How did you come to make shoes?"

He grinned up at her, "my mother."

"Was she a shoemaker?"

"No. After the accident, she couldn't wear shoes. She's the reason I learned to make shoes. You should meet her, you'd like her."

Rosa didn't ask how he knew that but guessed his mother was an advocate, or social worker, or something.

"As I learnt new things, I used her as my test subject."

"She must have a lot of shoes then."

"A few," he grinned, "not all of them successful. But each pair I make for her means I get better at making shoes for people like you."

He paused, and looked at her, his eyes darkening to chocolate again, "would you maybe like to go out for a drink sometime?"

"How about now?"

He smiled, a long slow smile she might have missed if she wasn't looking at him.

《《 • 》》

Not only did she say yes, but she suggested now! Jude did an imaginary happy dance.

She was easily the most intriguing person he'd ever met.

Stubbornly closed off and independent, with a hint of something softer inside.

Like bitter, dark chocolate with a gooey sweet caramel centre.

"This is just a way to avoid the pain of the massage, right?" he asked.

"Oh no, it's wonderful - you could do my whole body and I wouldn't complain."

He looked up at her face, a little flushed, lips parted, eyes brilliant.

The Rosa who'd walked in the door might have blushed and turned away, but something had happened to that Rosa, and this new Rosa looked at him boldly.

Challenging.

Her challenge pushed all the oxygen out of the room, and he was gasping for air.

Trying to remember why he shouldn't kiss her.

She leaned forward.

Just a fraction, but it was enough.

He reached out to grasp her arms, she fell into his embrace and kissed him.

He stopped thinking.

Sometime later, he pushed his hand up her leg, glossed over her bare hip and around her waist in a loose hug.

He kissed her shoulder and nuzzled her neck.

"About that drink?"

She rolled over to face him, cupping his face in her hand as she kissed him.

He tightened his grip, prepared to dally on the workshop floor a bit longer.

"Just a drink?" she said

"Actually, I was thinking about a bite of dinner as well."

"I could eat."

"At a restaurant? Or perhaps somewhere more intimate?"

"Did you have somewhere in mind?"

"There's a small Spanish restaurant in the Lane, we could get some tapas."

"I could eat tapas."

He masked a sigh with another kiss. He'd been afraid she wouldn't want to be seen in public with him.

Or worse, that she'd want to leave.

But he wasn't going to let her walk away without a fight.

"Can I help you dress?"

She froze for a moment, considering her options. Perhaps the bold Rosa had already left.

"Sure," she finally replied.

And a short while later, he realised the problem was the skinny jeans. Almost impossible to get into with any dignity remaining.

"Not much elastic in these suckers," he commented.

She laughed, "no. That day my clothes literally melted on my body, I'm not letting that happen again."

He paused to kiss a scar. "You've been through a lot."

"It could have been worse."

He wrapped her half-naked body in his arms, "you make me want to be a better man."

She accepted his tight hug, "you're already a better man than most.

"Now, about that dinner."

They quickly finished dressing.

As they left, he locked the door, and set the alarm.

"Was the door unlocked the whole time?"

He grinned, "yep."

"Anyone could have walked in anytime?"

"Yep."

"But..."

He paused to let her say more, and when she didn't, he kissed her again. "You're a bit of a daredevil, aren't you?"

"I hadn't for one moment thought you hadn't locked the door."

"To have locked the door when I came back would have been presumptuous."

She gave him a look that would have made lesser men quail, but he just laughed, took her hand and led her down the stairs.

The Spanish restaurant was delightful.

He ordered *mojitos*, olives, spicy chips, grilled eggplant and capsicum infused with garlic and parsley, *jamón iberico* and *chorizo* croquettes, and oysters.

They drank, and ate, and laughed.

She had a dry, acerbic sense of humour, and he wondered if she'd always been that way, or if it was a defence she'd picked up along the way.

And yet there was truth in her observations about life and people.

He covered her hand with his, and she didn't draw it away.

She tucked his hair behind his ear so she could see his face.

He leant across the table and kissed her.

《《 • 》》

Rosa stretched, and this time, her scars didn't pull her back.

She felt pleasantly stretched and exercised. Maybe there was something to the scar massage after all.

Or maybe there was something to him.

After dinner they'd walked to his art deco apartment, stopping for gelato on the way.

And she'd spent the night there.

His apartment was strangely calming. White walls, the bare essentials for furniture, and next to no clutter. Nothing to detract from the large, vibrantly coloured paintings on the wall.

Somehow, it was exactly like him.

And now, somehow, it was exactly like her.

The thought of returning to her cramped and claustrophobic apartment was horrifying.

It had been less than 24 hours since she'd met Jude Webb, but he had rescued her from her bleak existence.

After all that happened the day before, could she let him go?

She'd thought it would be easy, but he was under her skin now.

Rosa turned to speak to him, but the bed was empty.

She sat up and found the room was empty as well.

A door slammed, and she smelled coffee.

"I didn't know if you'd like a latte or an espresso, so I got both."

She grinned as he walked in with a cardboard tray of coffee, and a couple of pastries and sat on the bed.

"Latte," she said, "no sugar."

He twisted the tray so she could pick a coffee up, and after she'd taken her first sip, twisted it back to offer the pastry.

"Actually, I prefer a more savoury breakfast," she said taking a bite, "but somehow this is perfect."

He took a drink of his coffee, "must be the company," he said, toeing off his shoes and reclining on the bed next to her.

"'Spect so," taking another bite.

The last couple of years had been hard, and sitting there, in his bed, she realised that if she didn't take the chance, she would regret it forever.

Nothing ventured, nothing gained - wasn't that what they said?

"Do you have any plans for today?"

"Nothing I can't cancel," he said, "what did you have in mind?"

"Well, I might start with a long, hot shower, and see what happens. Would you care to join me?"

"I'm in," he said, "I'm all in."

THE END

CANCELLED BY THE CARTEL

Daisy Day paced the length of the faded green paisley carpet, her black patent heels thudding through what was left of the pile to echo in the sparsely furnished office.

She'd inherited the mahogany bookshelves, filing cabinets, desk and chairs along with the Director's Office from her predecessor, but he'd taken all the contents with him, and she saw no need for the fripperies fat old white men favour.

She theorised they enjoyed watching their secretaries dust them while they fumbled with their belts under the desks.

Her secretary, the young Miss Hawkins, had more important things to do than dust her baubles while she watched.

She realised she was smoothing the rough fabric of her navy-blue tweed suit in an attempt to hold the stress at bay and forced herself to fold her hands behind her back.

Yes, this week's Monday morning meeting was a BIG meeting with the new Department Head, but she was as prepared as she was ever going to be. All the files revised, all the problems highlighted, everything tickety-boo.

After a smart about-turn, she paced the length of the carpet again and picking up her lukewarm tea, looked out the window.

It was the kind of crisp, bright blue mid-winter day that teased you with the prospect of being warmer outside than it really was. She could almost smell a floral-scented breeze, though of course, you didn't get that in Summer in Melbourne let alone the Winter.

She held the saucer in her left hand, a little under her chin, and sipped from the cup in her right. Her fingers curled into her palm, balancing the weight.

None of that mucky-muck little fingers raised for her.

Pigeons circling in the nameless small park across the street carved shadow arcs across the faded blue and white floral wallpaper.

At least until some kind of falcon swooped and they scattered.

Raised voices in the corridor approached the door.

She cocked her head, Hawkins attempting to deflect Mr Pomfrey.

She sighed. And so it began.

Really, she was too old for this. She ought to retire and take a place out in the countryside. Get a dog and take it for long country walks.

Certainly, this was not the life she'd imagined when she was young.

She'd expected marriage and children. Greeting Don with his pipe and slippers when he returned from a hard day at the office.

And yet he'd been murdered in front of her.

Well, not actually in front of her. She'd been unconscious thanks to a sharp blow on the head, and who knew how long he'd survived after that.

Or what had been done to him.

She'd woken up in hospital several days later.

She could still remember the scent that preceded the blow; fog or more likely mist rising from the river, cigar smoke, supple leather, whisky and some kind of creamy shaving soap.

And now, like Miss Marple, she was a spinster; old and marginally relevant. Though having skipped the children and decades of Sunday dinners, still with her svelte shape intact.

She put the tea back on her desk and smoothed her hand across her immaculate salt and pepper chignon as she sat. Slipping her glasses on as she picked up a sheaf of papers to look busy.

The knock came almost before she was ready for it, and Pomfrey burst in before she acknowledged it. Followed by the distraught secretary.

Mercifully Pomfrey fell silent at her mildly reproving look. Over her spectacles and under her slightly frowning brow.

The older woman's weapon is to send grown men back to their childhoods with a disapproving face.

"I'm sorry Ma'am," Hawkins said, "Mr Pomfrey insisted."

Daisy waved her away with a small smile so she would know she wasn't to blame. The girl nodded, and leaving the door open, retreated to her desk outside the door.

"Pomfrey, why don't you take a seat?" she put her papers down, indicated the seats in front of her desk, and folded her hands.

The previous, Director had been a short man who'd sawn an inch or so off the chair legs, and Daisy hadn't seen a reason to swap them out.

With a name like Daisy Day, it had been hard enough to build credibility and rise to the rank of Section Chief, but she still needed all the help she could get when it came to dealing with patronising subordinates like Pomfrey.

He spluttered, knowing all about the chair situation. He'd been the kind of crony who'd enjoyed being in on the joke.

Daisy relaxed back into her chair, crossing one leg over the other.

Knowing he couldn't prevent himself from watching, she steepled her fingers under her chin and gently swung her top leg.

Waiting.

The man made a sound of annoyance and threw himself into a chair.

"I want to know what you're going to do about Soho."

Daisy considered his florid, too many drinks over too much lunch face and physique, the cigarette burn in his unfashionable tie, and his greasy Clarke Gable inspired side part with a pencil-thin moustache.

Should she humour him?

No. There were bigger fish to fry now.

Abruptly, she was annoyed with herself as well as him. She was better than him by a long shot.

She dropped both feel to the floor at sat up at her desk.

"That's no longer your concern."

She let his tirade wash over her while she considered what she was in fact going to do about Soho.

And Lord knew how it had become her problem when it was Pomfrey's bad judgement that brought them to this impasse.

Couldn't let him muck it up any further.

She stood up.

"That will do I should think. You've had your say, and I'll take it on board.

"Now," she rested her palms on the desk, stood up, leaning slightly to pick up her files for the meeting, allowing him to imagine cleavage through her high collared suit.

God, she was doing it without thinking. Men like Pomfrey were so easy to manipulate.

"I believe you have other matters to attend to, as do I."

It looked like he was planning to stay and argue some more, so she walked around her desk and gestured towards the door.

He shot out of his chair, clearly set on haranguing her all the way to wherever she was going, but at least he'd left the office.

She made a show of locking the door and pocketing the key, before walking away at a pace she knew he couldn't keep up with.

When exactly was it that handsome young men turned into ageing Pomfreys?

And why was it, that the more repulsive they became, the more voracious their appetites.

Taking the stairs, she left him wheezing in her wake, and two stories up he'd given up.

She took the opportunity to visit the ladies toilet; there were only two in the building, converted by replacing the male sign from the door with a female one.

She gave herself a thumbs-up sign in the mirror, adjusted the lie of her suit and moved on.

It seemed that the main reason for the Monday meeting was to compare notes about their weekend conquests. For the men in the room to detail their exploits in an attempt to embarrass her.

She didn't expect much aside from a couple of wasted hours. Nothing seemed to change, nothing seemed to get done, nothing really happened. Always the same meeting, regardless of new weeks or new faces.

It was possible they were playing her. Then again, they were complacent. Always thinking women were incompetent and easily bullied into submission.

When the Police Investigation into Don's death had stalled, or more likely, swept under the carpet, they'd told her to let it go and move on. They assured her she'd find another beau.

As if you could easily substitute one man with another and not tell the difference.

She hadn't been reassured, and she didn't want another beau, so she'd started her own investigation.

Astounded by what she'd found.

The lines of power and corruption seeped through Parliament, the public service, business and education.

Like any good business, the cartel took an early interest in bright young men and groomed them well.

All those jaded Pomfreys were once young men with stars in their eyes. Lured with a little dabble in this and a flirt with that, just enough to keep them eager and pliant.

Bending the rules a little, led to bending them a lot, until they were so compromised, they had nowhere to turn.

And those that fought back, like Don, left for dead on the way.

She couldn't believe they were so brazen, but at the same time, couldn't quite believe they weren't suspicious of her in the slightest.

Was it because she was a woman, therefore of no account, or that it was simple to arrange an "accident" and eliminate her on short notice?

Must be the bright, starry-eyed men who did that.

The Monday meeting was in the Department Head's office, with the other three Section Chiefs.

His office was similar to her own, only larger, with less filing cabinets and more knick-knacks.

And this week, two chairs behind the desk as well as the four in the front.

Not caring to contribute to the weekend conversation she reviewed her files, and tried to guess what either of the Heads might want to know.

Probably nothing going by other weeks. Either way, they were content for her to fix it and move on, or screw it up and take the fall.

And then Daisy smelled a familiar scent.

One she hadn't realised until that moment she'd been searching for across decades.

And suddenly she was back there by the Yarra River. Walking hand in hand along Flinders Walk. Convinced Don was about to propose to her.

Leaving her head bowed, she shut her eyes.

Could she be wrong about the scent?

She concentrated.

Creamy shaving soap? Check.

Cigar smoke? Check

Whisky? Check

The lack of river mist and leather could be down to meeting indoors rather than by the river.

Not enough to go on, she'd have to give him the benefit of the doubt.

She opened her eyes and watched the other section chiefs greeting him like a long-lost friend.

He was taller and thinner than them, dressed in an immaculately tailored charcoal suit, and possibly handmade black shoes as well.

Blond hair turning grey, grey eyes, clean-shaven, with an easy manner about him.

As his attention turned to her, she stood up.

Not a flicker of recognition.

A moment of sexual interest, gone almost as soon as it registered.

Could she use that to find out more about him? Like was he near the Yarra on that day?

The outgoing chief introduced her to the incoming.

"Miss Day, may I present Mr Carmichael. Carmichael, this is Daisy Day, Section Chief of Planning."

His hand was cool and dry as he enclosed hers within it.

"Miss Day."

"Mr Carmichael."

He turned away, effectively dismissing her as everyone else did.

"Please sit down everyone, I'll just be observing this meeting."

He picked up one of the chairs from behind the desk, and moved it a little way back and across, outside of the circle of chairs. Then leant back to pick a chestnut leather-bound notebook and a black and gold marbled fountain pen from the desk.

As the others began their weekly reports, Daisy looked at him from the corner of her eyes. He appeared intent on taking notes about the matters under discussion.

She took her own notes as the meeting progressed, but now as boredom set in, stole glances at him.

Sometimes she caught him boldly watching her and looked away.

Sometimes he caught her watching him, and she looked away then too.

That he looked at her, made her uncomfortable.

Not because it was sexual, though it was that too, but because he wasn't *overlooking* her.

She gave her report, and he didn't look at the walls or ceiling or carpet. He *looked* at her.

And she wasn't used to that at all.

After the meeting, she attempted her usual early exit, but Mr Carmichael blocked her exit, catching her arm.

She looked at his long, slim fingers circling her arm, and when he didn't withdraw them, glared up at him and wrenched her arm away.

He didn't let go.

"There's something about you Miss Day that makes me uneasy, and I intend to find out what it is."

"I expect you've been a naughty boy and I remind you of Nanny," she replied.

"Now, if you will excuse me, I have more pressing matters than your curiosity to attend to." She attempted to brush his hand loose.

He waited long enough for her to understand he'd let her go.

This time.

Next time, perhaps not.

Daisy left the room, back straighter than a poker, aware he was watching her.

Taking the stairs down, she knew that unlike Pomfrey, it would be damn near impossible to outrun him on the stairs.

Back in the relative safety of her own office, she folded her arms across her chest and looked out the window.

She could feel her heart pounding furiously in her chest.

Was it possible he recognised her from that night on the Yarra?

Conceivably whoever knocked her out had rolled over to check her pulse or that she was truly out of it and not faking.

She'd always assumed she'd been knocked out and left for dead, but was it possible something else happened to her while she was unconscious?

The thought made her shiver.

It had been days before she woke up in the hospital, had the cartel reached into the hospital to ensure she didn't wake up any sooner?

That any evidence from the river bank had been safely removed from her body as well as her clothes?

Or had she got it wrong, was she perhaps not supposed to wake up at all.

She shivered again.

Pacing her office wasn't going to cut this level of stress, she needed to walk it out.

There were some files to be delivered to another Department on the other side of the City. It might be a good idea to deliver them herself.

Maybe take a long walk by the Yarra to see that that kindled any further memories.

She put her coat on, told Hawkins where she was going and set off.

As she exited the building and started walking down the street, she felt her skin crawl.

There was nothing to hide, she didn't look back, yet the feeling someone was watching, or even worse following her, didn't subside.

She set a pace, just this side of a trot in case any Pomfreys were following her.

She dropped off the files, bought a drink she didn't want to drink and a sandwich she didn't want to eat to explain the pause, and sat on a bench by the river.

Quite close to where she'd been knocked out, about midway between the Princes and Queens Street bridges.

On an ordinary day, the slow-moving Yarra was calming.

Sunshine breaking randomly through the clouds. The occasional sound of a tourist boat's motor and horn as it puttered up or down the river, followed by a whiff of diesel. Swiftly diluted by the light breeze blowing upriver.

Today, it seemed one hundred and one seagulls squabbled on its surface. One thousand and one tourists took pictures or ate and drank in the restaurants lining the river's edge.

And unsurprisingly, Mr Carmichael seating himself beside her, sliding his arms along the bench, one almost touching the back of her neck.

"I thought I might find you here."

The hair on the back of her neck was standing on end, but she couldn't let him see how rattled she was, so she slid a little forward and away from his hand, opened her sandwich, and bit into it.

Managing not to spill any of it into her lap.

"Why of all the possible places in the City you might go, did you come here."

Still chewing, she gestured behind her.

He looked over his shoulder at the building behind her, its Departmental logo loud and proud across the facade.

She swallowed, "why are you following me."

He crossed one leg over the other, and gently swung it, much the same as she'd done to Pomfrey earlier that day, she looked at it like it was a tiger snake preparing to strike.

"I'm not following you," he said, "I have a meeting back there in about ten minutes."

There was nothing she could say to that, it had been her argument after all. She took another bite of her sandwich, knowing she couldn't ask him to leave without arousing his suspicion.

Knowing ordinary people didn't throw out lunches they'd barely eaten.

He sat in silence as she ate, lightly tapping the bench behind her with his fingers, leg still idly swinging.

Each mouthful was harder and harder to chew and swallow.

"It *is* a beautiful day by the river," he said, "it's a shame to go back to the office."

He edged a little closer to her, "what say we play hooky and go for a drink instead."

She edged a little further away, "what say we don't."

He looked at her and smiled, a genuine smile, so full of humour she almost forgot he could well be the person who killed her Don.

"You'd sentence me to the drudgery of another meeting after you couldn't wait to get out of the last?"

She choked on her sandwich and couldn't stop coughing. He patted her back and offered her a handkerchief for the tears streaming down her face.

She put the sandwich back into the paper in her lap, and found the napkin in her pocket, just in time to catch the food as it left her mouth.

Gasping for air.

He didn't stop patting her back, so she slid a little closer to the edge of the seat.

"Mr Carmichael. It's really not appropriate for you to be touching me during working hours."

His hand lay still on her back, burning through the thick wool of her overcoat. He leaned in, his scent strong in the close contact, "and after hours?"

"You're my boss, it's not appropriate ever."

"That's right," he said, "and I have a meeting to go to."

He stood up and grasped her shoulder firmly, but not painfully, "I'll be seeing you," then tapped her shoulder three times for good measure before he walked away.

Daisy sat on the bench, watching the river flow by.

Trying to decide whether he was flirting with her, or warning her.

Did he know something? Was he punching her buttons by design or coincidence?

Or did he just think she was an attractive and available female?

One night stand. Doubtful he wanted something longer term.

She scrubbed her face with her hands and sighed. There's a fine line between acceptable behaviour and harassment, sometimes impossible for both sides to navigate.

She sighed and looked at the sandwich in her lap. She hadn't wanted it before, and she definitely didn't want it now. And as for a "drink," well she could do with a shot of hard liquor right now too.

But not here where Carmichael, damn the man, might see.

She folded the paper back around what was left of her sandwich, dumped it in the closest bin, and started retracing her steps back to the office.

She paused outside her favourite bar for a long moment but pushed on back to work. She might need a drink right now, but she needed her wits about her more.

Her Pomfrey-evading tactics weren't going to work on Carmichael.

The rest of the day passed uneventfully, aside from expecting Carmichael to drop by and jumping every time there was a knock on the door.

By the time she'd reached the end of the day she was wound so tight she thought she might explode.

She took the train home and thought she saw him sitting in the next carriage.

Shopping for something for dinner at the supermarket, she thought she saw him at the meat counter.

And at her apartment building, as the lift door slid closed, a hand reached in triggering the safety and reopening the doors to reveal Mr Carmichael.

She looked up at his attractive, smiling face and couldn't quite grasp why he was there in her apartment building.

"Ah Miss Day," he said, "do you live in this apartment building too?"

She could only stare at him, eyes wide, jaw dropping.

"I've just moved back to Melbourne," he continued, "it'll be nice to know someone else here."

He turned to punch the button for his floor, and then turned back, "how wonderful, we're both on the fourth floor!"

Snap out of it NOW, she begged herself.

Somehow, she managed to stand upright, close her mouth and smile a straight lipped smile, "I'm not sure I would go so far as to say we know each other."

"Are you sure? You seem so familiar. I'm sure I've met you before."

"I'm sure I would remember you, and I don't."

He took a step closer, suddenly serious, "are you quite sure. Why don't you think back and tell me where we met?"

Daisy managed not to shrink back, "quite sure."

The lift dinged their arrival at the floor, and she took the opportunity to brush past him and walk to the end of the corridor where her flat was located.

"Oh look," he said catching up with her as she unlocked her door, "we're neighbours."

She opened her door and somehow managed not to slam it.

Dumping her shopping in the corridor, she went straight for the whisky bottle and got herself a large drink.

It seemed that in the space of eight hours, her life had turned to complete chaos through the introduction of Mr Carmichael.

He'd invaded her work, and by moving into the apartment next door, he'd invaded her personal life too.

By now, she was convinced he'd tried to kill her all those years ago. There were just too many coincidences for his appearance to be random happenstance.

The spectre of this had hung over her entire adult life, and now they wanted to ruin the small measure of peace she'd achieved.

She needed to choose; fight or flight?

She had a plan to disappear; cash and traveller's cheques secured in a small safe in her wardrobe. A bag was packed with a few clothes.

But now the time had arrived, and she was annoyed they thought they could bully her into submission.

As the rage moved through her body, she clenched her fists and bared her teeth. An edgy, twitchy feeling rose within her, and planting her feet wide apart, she roared with rage.

It wasn't fair.

She deserved the life that had been stolen from her, and she was damned if Mr Carmichael was going to steal this one too.

She'd always been upright and honest in her all dealings.

Never so much as accepting a glass of water from her clients, never rounding her time sheets up or down, never doing anything that might put her under obligation to another.

It was enough now.

It was time to end this once and for all.

To bring justice, not just for herself, but for all the others the cartel had brought low.

For the first time, she acknowledged to herself that she had been damaged by Don's death. That it was a gaping wound she had never got over.

If she wanted to live an ordinary life, she would have to heal that wound.

Even if she had to die trying.

And then she thought again.

Maybe it was simpler than that.

Maybe the answer was marketing.

Divide and conquer. Twitter campaigns. Cancel culture. Conspiracy theories.

Public Relations is, after all the best defence.

But she had to be clever about it.

She jumped when someone knocked on her door, though it sounded more like someone was beating on it with their fist.

She stepped over the shopping to open it.

"Oh thank God," Mr Carmichael said, "I thought something had happened when you screamed like that. I was going to get the Building Manager to open your door when you didn't answer."

She looked at him blankly. Noticing he had changed into jeans and a powder blue jumper that suited his colouring and brought a touch of colour to his eyes.

He put his hand on his heart, in what she thought was dramatic irony. "I was worried."

And then she understood.

It was all part of his campaign of destabilisation.

And she wondered how she might use this against him.

"It's been a tough day," she said, "would you consider a drink on the rooftop garden?"

"Oh," he said, caught off guard, "okay, sure."

"Let me get changed, and I'll meet you up there in fifteen minutes or so."

He backed up, away from the door. "Sure. Okay. I'll see you there."

She shut the door in his face.

Picking up her shopping, she dropped it in the kitchen on her way to her bedroom. Quickly changed into jeans and an old sweatshirt with a faded logo, then washed her face, pulled the pins from her chignon and combed her hair out with her fingers.

That felt better already.

She prepped some snacks and tossed them in an esky with a half-empty bottle of whisky.

Daisy wasn't sure what she hoped to achieve by inviting him to the roof. It wasn't like she could ask him if he'd killed her boyfriend twenty years ago.

She'd just have to play it by ear.

She arrived early, but he'd arrived earlier and spread his own picnic on the communal table closest to the edge of the roof.

The one behind the largest pot plants, that offered the greatest measure of privacy.

Fortunately, he'd remembered to bring glasses.

She knocked the first one back, breathing out the fumes.

It left a warm glow in her belly along with a dash of false bravado.

"That bad was it?" he asked, pouring her another drink.

She leant on the railing and looked at the ground. "There's this new guy at work, and the way that he follows me around gives me the creeps."

"Ah," he joined her at the railing. "Well, about that. I'm sure I know you from somewhere."

She swirled the drink around in her glass, "and what if you were doing something wicked at the time?"

"I'm fairly sure I have never done anything wicked."

She sipped her drink, and turned her back to the railing to look at him, "nothing you'd be ashamed to be seen in the newspapers for?"

"Nothing," he said emphatically.

"We'll see," she muttered.

"Sorry?" he leaned towards her

"Nothing.

"Hold this," she said, holding out her glass.

She pulled a hair elastic from her pocket and pulled her hair back into a ponytail. She hadn't intended to show him her scar, but as she turned her head, light glanced across the white threads marking her skin.

"Wait!"

He caught her arm and pulled her back into the light, exploring the web of scarring with gentle fingers.

Surprised, and angry, she pushed him back with both hands on his chest, and he fell into the parapet around the edge of the roof.

He flailed his arms, trying not to drop the glasses and leant on the rails as he tried to get back on his feet. But the railing broke and he started to overbalance.

For an instant she was frozen in place, not wanting to let him fall, and not wanting to save his life.

He let out a strangled cry, and she realised that no matter what he'd done, he didn't deserve to fall six storeys to the ground.

She reached out to take his hand, but he'd already lost his footing and was trying not to fall from the roof.

She lunged at him and managed to catch an arm as he overbalanced, falling to her knees and bracing herself against the concrete gutter.

He swung his other arm and managed to catch hold of the gutter.

"Hold on," she cried.

She tried pulling him further up, but couldn't shift him.

"You have to find a toehold or something to leverage yourself up."

"I can't."

"Don't be stupid. I can't hold you, and if you don't, you'll fall!"

"I can't."

She took a deep breath and held it, speaking through her gritted teeth, "there is no one here but you and me.

"No one is going to turn up in the nick of time to save you.

"The only person who can save you is you."

"I can't."

"You are the worst fucking evil bastard that ever walked this earth," she screamed, "and it would serve you right if I just let you go."

She braced herself, "in fact I'm going to let you go right now."

"Nooooo," he wailed, and finally she heard him scrabbling his feet against the wall of the building.

And suddenly he found a toe hold and launched himself up and over the gutter.

She was too slow to get out of the way, and he landed on her, rolling them both away from the edge, and coming to rest, lying by her side.

Both panting from the exertion.

"I know where I know you from now."

She didn't respond.

"I found you unconscious by the Yarra and called an ambulance. I went with you to the Royal Melbourne Hospital emergency department."

She turned her head to look at him.

"I waited while they operated on you, and put you into a coma. I only left you because I had a flight to catch, and when I got back, you'd gone."

"What about Don?"

"Don? Who's Don?"

"He was my boyfriend who turned up dead."

He turned to look at her, "you were on your own. No one else was with you."

Daisy looked up at the sky. That changed things a bit.

Had Don been part of the cartel?

Had *he* been the one who bludgeoned her?

Had she been wrong about him all along?

And to cap it all, had he actually died?

"Anyway, I'm glad you made a full recovery."

She looked at him again, "yeah, I'm fine aside from 20 years of excess baggage."

He snorted, "I think I need a drink."

"Sounds good to me. Can you get up?"

He groaned as he elbowed himself to a sitting position, and groaned some more as he used a pot plant to pull himself upright.

He stood swaying, then offered her his hand, "I'm sorry if I came on too strong today."

She took his hand and he pulled her upright, she stumbled as she overbalanced into him.

"Oop," she said, "I thought you might have been the person who murdered Don."

"Ah, that explains your initial reaction. "What gave you the idea?"

"Your cologne."

He let her loose. "I'm afraid we lost the glasses, care to share the bottle?" he offered it to her first.

She sat down and took a swallow, making a guttural noise as the alcohol hit the back of her throat, and offering him the bottle back.

He sat down, looking out over the night sky, bottle dangling between his legs. "What now?"

"I'm sorry I pushed you."

"Not your fault the railing chose that moment to fail."

She sighed, "I don't know what to think anymore. The hatred I felt for the people who murdered Don has controlled me for too long, yet I can't see another way to look at it all."

He took another swig of the bottle and handed it back to her. "What will you do?"

"Just keep going. Get up and go to work, and pretend like it's another ordinary day."

"No need to rush. Take a day off."

"Shouldn't that be my line? You're the one who's just had a near-death experience."

"Maybe we should take a day at the beach. Wash our cares away."

"It's the middle of winter!"

"Best time. No one there."

He grinned, and she started laughing.

And didn't stop for a long time.

THE END

THE SECOND SON SQUAD

I didn't know where I was, and I didn't know how I got there.

I do know I am, or used to be; a top-notch accountant working for one of the global corporations.

Some might say I am, or was, was one of the most ruthless.

And if some of those knew where I was now, they might say I had it coming to me.

I am now in the body of a teenage girl, who is pretending to be a boy, in an old and elite Military Academy that churns out highly regarded Officers in training.

And it's not like I don't have any urgent issues of my own to manage instead of being wherever the hell I am.

There's money to be cleared through tax havens, gift payments to be made, deals to funnel through shelf companies and trusts.

Exploiting loopholes doesn't just happen by itself.

I think I'm somewhere in Eurasia, but I don't know exactly where. Going by the fashions, I think I'm some time around the turn of the century, say 1910 or maybe 20.

But I don't even know whether I'm on the same planet, or some near-Earth alternative. Geography was never my strong suit.

Somehow, I find being trapped in a near Earth environment more acceptable than having time travelled into another body.

If I believed in reincarnation, I might be inclined to think she is some kind of ancestor. But I only believe in science, so I'm more inclined to believe your consciousness terminates and your body rots.

Or doesn't depending on the embalming.

Regardless, it seemed logical to me, that I needed to resolve whatever unfinished business I found myself in the thick of before I could get back to my own life and resolve the issues that could land me in jail, or dead in a ditch somewhere.

My name was Abby Fisher, but the boys call me Ting Ting, because that, apparently, is the sound a bullet would make ricocheting around my empty head.

Even the Instructors call me Ting Ting, because that's also the sound a thought would make ricocheting around my empty head.

At that stage, I had no idea what my body's actual name was.

Nor why she enrolled in the Military Academy, though it may have had something to do with the partially blurred photo of a young man she keeps hidden in her trunk.

Ting Ting was very bad at almost all military things. Except martial arts training where her small size was more of an asset, and marksmanship.

She was the slowest person on the obstacle course; hopeless at climbing over walls and crawling under barriers. Not too bad on the balance, hopeless at the rope ladder and net.

The boys tease her about the time she passed out in a puddle of muddy water.

I suppose I'm not good at that stuff either, though her times have improved since I got here. If Ting Ting's muscles have any memory, she certainly isn't sharing it with me.

Though I did use to enjoy kicking the shit out of people at the dojo, so who's to say she was any good at martial arts either.

Similarly, once I'd adjusted for the rifle noise, weight, and recoil, shooting the paper target was as easy as shooting zombies or robot killing machines in the arcade games.

She has a deep well of rage. It consumes her. It could just be puberty kicking in; I know I was full of rage at that age too. But I get the sense it's a deep and abiding rage; something tightly held and generously nurtured.

Revenge, cold, all that shit.

Since I woke up in her body, my resting bitch face has become her asset too. Seemingly I could drop a man at 50 paces.

Resting bitch face or not, I was worried about being discovered. Theoretically, that would've just meant expulsion from school. But a young woman on her own out there isn't safe.

Rumours are rife with this faction bombing cities, and that faction sending spies and assassins, and the other factions killing civilians, raiding newspaper offices and killing journalists.

I read in the newspaper that a girl's school on the other side of the City held a peaceful protest, and whatever faction sent troops in to kill them all as a lesson to the rest of us.

Here in the Academy, I share a dormitory and a bathroom with the four boys who make up the rest of my unit.

Josh is the strategist and notionally the unit leader. He gets the bed; we get the bunks. He takes his training seriously, thinks deeply about the scenarios presented in the lectures, and can be relied on to do the right thing. But he's not much good at thinking outside the box.

I sleep on the bottom bunk, on your left as you walk in the door.

Nate sleeps on the top bunk, above my bed. He's the unit's funny guy, a little short, a little overweight, though I thought with the rations and exercise combined, he wouldn't stay that way. If anyone was going to short-sheet your bed, it would've been him.

Zac's in the other top bunk. He already has a body full of scars. He's the one who always runs headfirst into danger without thinking. I thought he'd be the first one killed. Probably in some kind of useless way.

And then there's Locky on the bottom bunk opposite my bed. He's beautiful, tall and blond, with muscles well-concealed within in a layer of thinness. He's so sharp he might cut himself. Sometimes I'd catch him looking at me, and could see his brain moving. I didn't think it would take him long to figure out my secret.

I'm pretty sure they're all boys, our dormitory certainly smells like teenage boys, and I thank god the windows open.

We all make a big show of shaving though I didn't expect any of us have stubble worth the name. I know I don't.

Ting Ting is a little underfed, and not well endowed in the bust department. With her slightly oversize uniform, I think she could get away without binding her chest, though she probably doesn't agree.

And who's to say she's not right, she probably knows the men and boys in this place better than I.

I've been here for a couple of weeks now. I've been following the boys around as I familiarised myself with the layout of the Academy, and worked out where the offices are and where the records are kept.

I say following, but not a lost dog kind of following, more like a kind of lazy, slouchy, dawdling which has resulted in a number of late marks and mild physical punishments.

I've also been sneaking out of the dorm at night, prying into the offices and records which are ridiculously unsecured. Though I suppose aside from spies and 21st-century women, a Military Academy doesn't have anyone to fear.

Firstly, I was trying to find out what Ting Ting's name was, and whether anyone knew she was female.

Secondarily, I was also looking for whatever it was she'd been looking for. Not that I had any idea what that might be.

One night I was sneaking through the school, and I came across Locky standing so still and silent I almost didn't see him.

He was completely unfazed to see anyone else in the corridors out of hours, putting his finger to his lips to indicate I should be silent.

I glided across to where he was standing, and at that point, I could hear conversation from the room behind him too.

"But no one knows where Darcy Dimes is," I recognised the voice of Sargent Walker the commander in charge of the obstacle course.

"It doesn't matter where she is," Sargent Sloane, the strategy lecturer said, "the people will rally around the idea of her."

"Will they?" Walker asked, "Will they really?"

"Of course they will; a princess is a princess is a princess. It doesn't matter whether she's next in line for the throne, or one hundredth," Sargent Thomas, the one in charge of administration and records said, "people will follow her."

I was about to move on; a conversation about princesses had no interest for me at that time, but Locky grabbed my wrist in a vice-like grip and didn't let go.

I looked up at him, his eyes were boring into mine, as cold as the chill in the air.

He wanted me to hear this conversation, and he wanted me to know he'd heard it.

I looked away and wondered was he someone known to me.

Did he think I was Darcy Dimes, whoever this princess was?

I suppose hiding a princess in a Military Academy made a certain kind of sense, but I had no doubt I wasn't Darcy Dimes.

I had a nebulous photo of someone to prove I wasn't a princess. Because carrying a photo of some guy isn't what princesses are known for.

Not that I had found any evidence to suggest who he was. Aside from not being a person currently living in the Academy.

Though there was a small cemetery within the grounds. I'd visited it, but aside from the names and dates of birth and death, I couldn't tell if he was there, because I didn't know his name.

Those that were interred, had all been young, and I wondered if the Academy was more ruthless than I had guessed.

As the days went by, I discovered it was a good place for thinking, to remind myself that Ting Ting, Abby Fisher, and everyone else paid, one way or another, for the lives they led.

And as I subsumed myself into Ting Ting's character, what the consequences might be for me.

I was recalled to my senses by Locky's sharp tug on my arm, just in time to not fall in a heap and get dragged behind him into an alcove a little further down the corridor.

I risked a peek and saw the Instructors filing out of the room. I was curious about Sargent Thomas; I wasn't in any of his classes. I think they were about how to write adequate reports of engagements and incidents. And other conscientious detail-oriented information mentioned in dispatches.

Whereas the other Instructors were lean and seemingly battle-ready, Thomas' physique was more along the lines you'd expect from someone who sat on their arse for a good deal of the day. And I would've wagered he ate perhaps more food than was strictly wise for a non-commissioned officer.

In fact, he reminded me a bit of that weasel Cunningham. I mean it's all very well to have a few gigs on the side, but to expect me to cover up his wrongdoings as well as those of his mafioso boss was a bit much.

Unfortunate then, that he'd caught me in a dalliance with the mafioso's eighteen-year-old son and now had leverage.

Not a sufficiently valid reason to be suspicious, but I reckoned steering clear of Instructor Thomas would be a good thing.

But back to Locky, pressed up against me in the dark, shadowed alcove as the Inspectors filed past.

I knew he was 15, maybe 16 at most. And despite my appearance, I was a thirty-year-old woman.

Who missed her boobs, which was kind of odd as I'd always said I'd get rid of them in an instant.

And without my boobs in the way, he was standing too close. Because I was masquerading as a boy I wondered if he was gay.

And then I wondered if he knew about Ting Ting and thought she couldn't escape him.

And then I realised I had to get away from him before I did anything I might regret.

I slid out from between the wall and his body and scarpered.

But oddly enough, the half-heard conversation about Princess Darcy Dimes stayed with me.

Maybe I felt sorry for her because she was a girl trapped in a life she didn't want. Not unlike me.

Then again, Matilda, the daughter of Henry I hadn't been backwards about coming forwards in pursuit of the English throne.

Hadn't she fled to Normandy on her defeat?

Was the Academy pro or anti-Darcy?

Was she the legitimate heir?

After another exhausting day of lectures and obstacle courses, I went to the library to find out more.

I got out my notebook and skimmed through a bunch of newspapers to find out more about the current political situation. Taking notes where it seemed appropriate.

Externally, there were a number of religious groups, supported by a number of countries.

Internally, the King had been assassinated before I got there, leaving one direct heir, the Princess Darcy who'd gone into hiding.

The remainder of the large and sprawling Royal Family had separated into factions in support of assorted male claimants.

No wonder Princess Darcy had gone into hiding; she appeared to be the key to many a claim, and it wasn't hard to imagine her being forced into marriage to some arsehole bent on running the country, if not the world.

What a shit-storm.

The country had more or less broken into a bunch of city-states.

Princess Darcy was well off out of it.

But.

With my own history of corruption, I wondered about the other major players.

So, I started looking into them.

Oddly enough, my unit comprised sons of the nobility. Josh, Nate, Zac and Locky; all second sons of Dukes or Barons.

I opened a fresh page in my notebook and started tracing the lineages and loyalties.

My unit's fathers formed an interesting web of alliances and enemies such that theoretically, each of the four boys aligned into two pairs of "friends" and "enemies."

And that suggested the unit was formed by design, not coincidence.

Not for the benefit of the boys, but to produce a team their fathers would accept as representing their interests.

All claims to pre-eminence were countered by the others, in terms of rank, they were roughly equal.

I didn't know if it was odd they'd be in a unit together, but it suggested that whoever Ting Ting was, she was impersonating a younger son as well.

The tie-breaker, if you will.

But wouldn't they have known each other? At the very least by reputation, if not having met.

And if they'd known each other, did they also know Ting Ting's actual identity?

Was she really the Princess?

And if she was, did that make me a Princess?

Nothing would suffice, but to open the book at the page describing the King's children.

I kept my eyes closed for the longest time, summoning my courage, before opening them and looking into Darcy's face.

Thank god it wasn't the one I'd looked at while pretending to shave that morning.

That meant I was a decoy.

In the worst case, expendable.

In the best, in training to be a bodyguard or body double for Darcy, with my aristocratic unit.

If we lived that long.

On the bright side, also on the page was the blurred picture I had in my luggage. The deceased

Crown Prince who had died in mysterious circumstances a few years ago.

Did I know him?

Was that why I was here?

Locky, or more correctly, the Right Honourable Mr Lachlan Price sat opposite me. "So Lady Abigail, do you remember who you are now? Or why you're here?"

I looked at him.

Hard.

Not one flicker of memory from before I arrived. And any number of hurtful incidents since then.

I lifted my chin, "no, and no."

"That's a great shame," said The Right Honourable Mr Nathaniel Harrison, taking the seat next to Locky. "Keeton's making his move."

"Ah," I said, "Keeton's the one with the money."

"What does that have to do with anything?" asked The Right Honourable Mr Joshua Gatrell, pulling out the seat at the table next to us, spinning it on one leg, and sitting on it backwards.

"Well," my accountant's brain kicked in, "on the one hand he can afford hired mercenaries and assassins, on the other, they're only loyal as long as they keep getting paid."

"How does that help us," asked The Right Honourable Zachariah Turney leaning against the table and crossing his arms.

"All we have to do is interrupt the cash flow and we can bring the faction down."

They looked at me like I was nuts.

And who the hell did I think I was kidding?

How were five teenagers without computers going to achieve anything?

And then Locky said, "I dunno, that might work."

He grabbed an atlas from a nearby shelf and brought it back to the table. He flipped through the pages, then spread it open to the page showing the larger cities across wherever-the-hell it was we were.

"Keeton's chosen the mountain town of Tillia as his base," he said, tapping the location on the map. "He's going to need gold to pay his armies, and the only way it can get there is through the Overhand Pass—"

"And the Overhand is notorious for bandits," Zac said, leaning in to look at the map.

"Call that option B," said Josh, extricating himself from the chair and coming to stand looking down at the map as well. "Who's backing him might be a more important question."

I looked at my notes, "Blaxland, Temby and Semmens."

"That's just the public ones," said Nate, standing up to look at the map, "what about Pusey and Hallam?"

I sat back in my chair and watched them; heads bent over the map talking about how they could put the frighteners on the Lords.

And that's when I realised, they weren't talking about doing it themselves.

Keeton might be buying his army, but these second sons had resources they could draw against - lands, men, armaments. None of it technically theirs, but available for the greater glory of the King.

Or should I say Princess?

And in support of her, the gambit of something for the family, but also perhaps the grant of nobility for themselves.

When the Princess came to power, she would inevitably confiscate lands and maybe put a bunch of people to death. And when it came to the winners, well, she might grant my second sons the titles, lands and people she'd confiscated from others.

And what about me?

While they organised the work and allocated it through their families to take care of, I looked myself up in the book.

Actually, I was using the index, so I looked up five other Abigails before I found Lady Abigail Montrose.

Who went nuts and was committed to an asylum. Her photo showed a woman with a repulsively smug smile, and I wondered if it was taken before or after the asylum.

Before or after she went nuts with grief over Prince Hugo's death.

Before or after she escaped to the Military Academy.

Fairy Tales never tell you about the people trampled by the romance of the main narrative.

And what about me?

Would I go back home and try to extricate myself from the mess I'd got myself into?

Or would I be back in Abigail's asylum looking at the walls?

I frowned as I looked at "my" biography, bottom lip wobbling.

Given the choice, I wasn't sure what I'd pick. Would I get the choice?

What if I was already dead, and this was my karma playing out

Most likely, if I stayed here, I'd be a pawn in some kind of political play. Which actually wasn't that much different to what was happening in my actual life.

I heaved a sigh.

Locky touched my shoulder to get my attention, "are you okay?"

I glanced up at him to see his look of concern.

In fact, they were all looking at me.

With varying levels of sympathy and concern.

A single tear escaped my bleary eyes, and I ran for it. Up the stairs to the second story, back to the classrooms, and into a toilet cubicle.

I really needed a nice glass of red wine. Or failing that, a big block of chocolate.

It shouldn't have been a surprise Ting Ting had got her period.

And given she had no control over her diet, and wasn't taking the pill, that it was uncomfortable. I'm sure some things would have been available had she hidden out in a girl's school, but not in a Military Academy.

And it wasn't like I could stay in the toilet for the next few days, so there was nothing for it, but to get back to the dorm without being noticed, and see what else was in the trunk that might be useful.

I made it to the door of the toilets and found my-self on the wrong end of a blunt instrument.

Some time later, I found myself alone in a luxuri-ous bedroom.

By which I mean, lots of space, carpets on the floor, hangings on the walls, a fire crackling merrily in the hearth, a table and chairs, and a lot of bedding.

Sounds cushty, and it was, but the last bed I'd got out of was in amongst four boys, with basically farts and the closed door to keep us warm.

I couldn't help but be deeply suspicious of who-ever had brought me here.

And who had taken my clothes, dressing me in some kind of nightie, and leaving me with a dress and a bunch of complicated-looking undergarments?

Rude.

I checked the window, which appeared to be in a tower, and I was no Rapunzel. And the door was locked from the outside. I checked the window again, this time with a view to escaping from it, with next to no further inspiration.

It really wasn't looking good.

There was a knock at the door, and a woman en-tered with a tray of breakfast things. Outside I saw a soldier, not looking in my direction in case he saw something.

Which suggested that I was someone important, and whoever had brought me here was powerful. And knew who Lady Abigail was.

The woman with the breakfast tray deposited it on the table and gestured at it, then bowed and left the room. I ducked after her, but as expected, two soldiers barred my way. I didn't see any other signs of opponents in the corridor, but it wasn't long, and the soldiers backed me into the room without talking.

If I was a stronger person, I might not have eaten. But I was starved, and there was fresh bread and some kind of jam and some fruit.

Not enough to stick to my ribs and give me strength, but enough to tide me over until I could get something else.

I wolfed the food down, and ignoring the complicated bits, got dressed.

I had no idea what was coming, but I needed to stay calm and keep my wits about me.

In the Academy, we'd been learning to meditate; to focus on our breathing and detach the mind from emotions. To develop a directed concentration and a nonjudgmental awareness of the present.

The aim being to stay calm, focused on the moment, and survive in combat situations.

So, with nothing else to do, I closed my eyes, calmed my mind, and focused on the things I could control.

That being me.

Not long later, the woman came back and bullied me into dressing properly.

Then the soldiers escorted me down the long, winding staircase to the mostly empty great hall.

Where I came face to face with Keeton.

He gripped my shoulders firmly and kissed both my cheeks. Clearly, he and Ting Ting had some kind of relationship.

Which threatened my calm mind for a moment. Especially as he reminded me of that mafioso guy back in my universe.

But soon I was sorting through the implications.

Was I in Tillia?

Had Keeton got word of our plan?

Which one of my boys was the mole?

Keeton escorted me to a table in the centre of the hall with a firm hand on my back. He poured two glasses of wine and gave one to me.

"A toast my dear," he said, raising his glass toward me "to the woman who killed Prince Hugo," and took a sip.

I was in shock, and took too big a gulp of wine and started choking on it. Keeton pounded my back.

"I forgot my dear, you're not much of a drinker, are you? It's one of the things I like about you."

Holy fuck! Not only had I killed the Crown Prince, but I was neck-deep in putting Keeton on the throne.

And there I was thinking I was on the side of right. That someone else was the mole when all along it was me.

Psycho-bitch.

I'd known in my heart that I was too corrupt to be on the side of right. But wouldn't it have been great, just once, to be one of the good guys.

If my second sons knew who I was, were they all traitors as well?

Those poor, sweet, doomed boys.

But wait.

On the assumption I was pro Princess Darcy, we'd plotted out an attack on Keeton. And if they held it together after my kidnapping, it might still be going ahead.

And from what I'd read, Keeton seemed like the kind of guy who stays well back when the fight's on, then strolls in to take the credit.

So, were we "safe" in Tillia?

And could I get away, back to the academy, where I could redeem myself in the eyes of the others?

First things first, I had to get away from Keeton.

Which was actually fairly easy.

One last pound on the back and I vomited up the wine on him. When he tried to jump back out of the way, he knocked my arm, and I spilt the rest of it on both of us.

And landed on my knees in the worst of the mess, and then fell to my hands and knees and apologised profusely for the mess.

I thought for a moment he was going to kick me, and I have no doubt that he would have if I wasn't still useful to him.

But it suited his vanity to have a woman on her knees before him, so he sent me away to change and rest for dinner.

And while it would have served her right to marry him, I really hoped, just in case I was still here, that he wouldn't have her.

He left in a swirl of sandalwood scented finery, neglected to instruct anyone to take care of me, and therefore I became no one else's business.

I made my way to the basement on the assumption the laundry would be near there, and I was lucky enough to find some unattended clothing.

Not lucky enough to find clean clothing, but now that I knew I was a killer, I knew I deserved nothing more than someone else's filthy clothing.

I folded up something like a loin-cloth and changed my clothes.

And looking like some filthy boy, it was ridiculously easy to leave the castle.

Surely someone should have been watching?

Then again, I can't say the Academy actually encouraged independent thinking of any kind.

I'd been hoping to sneak away, follow the path down the mountain, and eventually find a train that would take me back to school, but I realised I had no idea where it was.

Nor did I know the name of the Academy.

Which put a bit of a crimp in my escape plan.

Should I hang around in my disguise in the hope of finding something to sabotage?

Or would my impromptu action harm the second sons' plan?

I was so angry at myself for being a traitor, I just wanted to burn the building down.

I wondered if I could find the armoury, or more particularly, the powder magazine. I started looking around for it.

The powder would need to be kept dry, and well away from anything that might create a spark. It would need thick walls, and possibly a reinforced roof. Or maybe it would be partially buried.

If you were sensible, it would be in an isolated position a little way away from the castle.

If you were less than sensible, you might leave it loose in the basement.

Either way, it didn't seem likely I'd be able to set fire to it without losing my life.

Then again, what about cartoon physics? Couldn't I set a fuse by knocking a hole in a keg and drawing a long line of powder? Theoretically yes.

And how would I light it?

Pipe smoking was common, could I steal a lit pipe, tap the embers out on the trail of gunpowder and make a run for it?

As good a plan as any. All I needed to do now was to figure out how to carry 75 litres of gunpowder.

I ruled out strapping it to an animal immediately.

And that meant I needed someone to help.

In the stronghold of my enemy, I needed someone to help me blow it sky-high.

Jesus wept, as the mafioso's girlfriend might say.

All right, I told myself, calm down.

Take a deep breath, calm yourself, and detach yourself from emotion. Just watch the people milling around you, and let your intuition guide you.

I spotted a little hut not far away that was probably it.

I looked for guards and became aware of a boy on the other side of the yard, who appeared to be looking at me. He was filthy but in the kind of way that looked like he'd dabbed on a bit of dirt as if it was makeup.

He looked kind of familiar.

He looked like Locky.

I flashed our secret signal gesture, and he flashed it back.

Thank god.

I shrugged my shoulder in the direction of the powder magazine, and he started walking over there.

I checked no one was following him, then started walking in that direction too.

We looked at each other for what seemed like forever.

"What's the plan?" he asked.

I sketched it out for him, and he looked doubtfully at me but shrugged his shoulders.

"Let's give it a go."

"Are the others with you?"

"No. We've got a mole and I didn't want to take any chances."

"Ah.

"I found out who it is," I said, "and it's me."

He said nothing for a moment.

"You've changed recently, and I can't put my finger on what it is, so I'm going to trust you. But if you've betrayed us, I will kill you myself."

I was tempted to make a joke about his battle training, but I said, "better you than anyone else."

It made me feel slightly better for it to be him; he was an excellent shot and I wouldn't suffer.

I couldn't believe we managed to get it all set up without anyone noticing anything out of the ordinary.

My shoulders were itching the entire time, waiting for someone to fire a shot into my back.

There were so many things that could have gone wrong with the plan I was loathe to leave it. But I couldn't let Locky sacrifice himself for my stupidity.

He lit the fuse, and I grabbed his hand and started running.

Down the bailey, through the curtain wall, across the drawbridge, and on our way down the mountain.

I thought my lungs would explode by the time I felt the ground rumble and felt the shock wave knock me off my feet.

《《 • 》》

I didn't know where I was, or how I got there.

I was in a white room, and Nuns I guess they were, were tending my wounds.

Which were extensive.

I'm told Queen Darcy visited me in my room and had helped tend my wounds before she passed her judgement.

For the murder of her brother, my penalty was death.

For the decimation of her main rival, and promotion to Queen, my penalty was commuted to life.

Not at the asylum, and not at the Nunnery.

Cast out to live alone on some island in the middle of a lake.

No doubt when I was more myself, whichever self that was, there would be some kind of paper documenting the punishment.

I wasn't upset about it, in fact, I was looking forward to it. A really nice long spell of time on my own. To think, and maybe write.

But that wasn't it at all.

According to the Who's Who, Lady Abigail Montrose the Prince Killer was dead. No doubt about it, blown up at Keeton's Castle thanks to the bold plan of the second sons.

But, the Queen had given me a new identity.

The Honourable Lady Ava Price, Lachlan's long-lost cousin.

And the new Ting Ting had a place at the Academy for the next term too.

I'm not sure why I'm still here.

But I'm going to enjoy it while it lasts.

THE END

ABOUT THE AUTHOR

Alexandria Blaelock writes stories, some of them for *Ellery Queen's Mystery Magazine* and *Pulphouse Fiction Magazine.*

She's also written four self-help books applying business techniques to personal matters like getting dressed, cleaning house, and feeding your friends.

She lives in a forest because she enjoys birdsong, the scent of gum leaves and the sun on her face. When not telecommuting to parallel universes from her Melbourne based imagination, she watches K-dramas, talks to animals, and drinks Campari. At the same time.

Discover more at www.alexandriablaelock.com.

www.ingramcontent.com/pod-product-compliance
Lightning Source LLC
Chambersburg PA
CBHW071019180726
48291CB00004B/1537